## BLITHE SPIRIT

The ghost took tiny steps toward him until she teetered on the very edge of the bed. Her hand lowered to meet his.

Their fingertips just inches apart, he gazed up at her. He felt like an adoring acolyte at the foot of a goddess's statue. This free, lost spirit had already captured him. Her eyes seemed to sparkle.

It was impossible he would feel anything but icy air if he touched her, but he felt compelled to try. Without thinking, he reached up and offered steadying support.

Their hands grasped, ice becoming warm flesh, and his world turned upside down.

# Touched by Time

## *Leanne Shawler*

## ZEBRA BOOKS
### Kensington Publishing Corp.
www.kensingtonbooks.com

ZEBRA BOOKS are published by

Kensington Publishing Corp.
850 Third Avenue
New York, NY 10022

All Kensington titles, imprints, and distributed lines are available at special quantity discounts for bulk purchases for sales
promotion, premiums, fund-raising, educational, or institu-
tional use.

Special book excerpts or customized printings can also be cre-
ated to fit specific needs. For details, write or phone the office
of the Kensington Special Sales Manager: Attn. Special Sales
Department. Kensington Publishing Corp., 850 Third Avenue,
New York, NY 10022. Phone: 1-800-221-2647.

Zebra and the Z logo Reg. U.S. Pat. & TM Off.

ISBN 0-8217-7830-7

First Printing:  July 2005
10 9 8 7 6 5 4 3 2 1

Printed in the United States of America

*For Dan,*
*and for my Mum,*
*who bought me books*
*instead of lollies*
*when I was good as a little girl.*

# Chapter One

*Bath, August 1812*

His world was perfect.

Ramsay Chadwick smiled graciously at his hostess and strolled about the large drawing room. At one time, he'd never have been allowed within Bath's *beau monde* circles, and yet here he was.

Thanks to his mother's fortune and nobility, combined with his father's good business sense, the family's wealth had more than doubled, rendering them visible in the eyes of Bath's gentry. Better yet, he'd sought and won the position of Bath magistrate.

Best of all, Miss Lydia Devereaux, the most beautiful girl in all of Bath, had agreed to be his wife. The wedding was fourteen days away. Not that he was counting.

He hummed under his breath, pausing to listen in appreciation to the trio hired this evening. The violins sang of his joy, of his success.

His future held a satisfying occupation, a gorgeous wife, and a country estate that would firmly establish him and his descendants as being of consequence.

Ramsay moved on from the musicians, his thoughts returning to his magisterial duties. A gentleman could be useful as well as decorative.

Unlike his closest friend, Mark Darby. He smiled upon spotting him at the edge of the crowd, dressed impeccably in the highest fashion and leaning in to try and steal a kiss from some pretty miss.

He watched as Darby failed, but that failure seemed due to propriety forbidding such an action in public rather than his lack of charm. The girl flirted with his friend, he detected, even though he saw little more of her than her fan and her skirt.

Parting, the couple exchanged looks full of secret promises.

Ramsay's breath choked in his throat, pain flashing through his chest.

Lydia.

His perfect world froze and shattered.

*Present Day*

If she never saw another man, it would be too soon.

Jane Leighton followed Mrs. Marshall, the owner of Chadwick's Bed and Breakfast, up the steep stairwell, the seagrass matting crunching under her feet.

This is what she needed, she told herself, drinking in the clean classic lines of Georgian design. She needed to get away from the grit of London, from her pathetic, clingy ex-boyfriend, and find peace and quiet. She needed to make plans, plans that didn't involve a man for once.

What better place to do that than in Bath? Its architectural perfection, mellowed with age, made the perfect background for figuring out what she wanted to do with the rest of her life. She couldn't foresee giving up her jewelry shop, but something had to change in her personal life.

Mrs. Marshall's ample girth made it impossible to see what lay ahead during their ascent. A jumble of pictures framed in black wood hung on the soft ivory painted walls. Some were smudged ink drawings of Bath, others reproductions of Hogarth's satirical series on the *Comforts of Bath*. As she lugged her suitcases, she promised to return and examine them.

Mrs. Marshall made the sharp 90-degree turn at the landing. Reaching the final stair, Jane glanced up. She gasped. A large painting of a man dominated the wall before her, the sheer opulence of the colors stopping her in her tracks.

This picture was no pale, flat print but the real deal, an authentic painting from . . . She tilted her head, evaluating the man's well-tailored attire that clung to his body like a second skin. Definitely the Regency. It should be in a museum, she thought.

More than the rich color held her. The artist, whoever he'd been, had had a gift. With his oils, he'd communicated the subject's tightly controlled vibrancy. His face seemed lit with excitement while holding a rigid frown. His carrot-red hair was smoothed along his scalp. His skin appeared white against the dark background of his library.

In one hand he held a scroll. The other pointed to a statuette of Justice. Had he just passed the bar? She got the impression he had been quite an imposing man.

Mrs. Marshall retraced her steps. "That's Ramsay Chadwick, one of the early owners of this house."

"He's cute." She answered Mrs. Marshall's beaming smile with a small one of her own. She couldn't deny it, even if she had given up men.

He wasn't conventionally handsome if you considered the Byronic model, but he was most definitely good looking. *Oh, yes.*

She wondered if it would be completely out of line to lean in close enough to determine the color of his eyes, as the age of the portrait had rendered them dark. She struggled to retain some semblance of modesty, lowering her bags for a moment. "You named your B&B after him?"

The owner nodded. "His story is the most interesting." She peered over her small spectacles. "Are you sure you don't need a hand with those bags?"

Jane shifted her grip on the leather handles, shouldering the weight again. "No, I'm fine."

Mrs. Marshall resumed her ascent of the stairs, talking about Ramsay Chadwick. "It's the best tale because it's the most tragic. He disappeared after his fiancée went tragically missing. So young and so beautiful. There's a portrait of her in the dining room downstairs. Whether Mr. Chadwick was her murderer or a fellow victim, unrecovered, is still open to debate." Her hostess took a breath. "You don't believe in ghosts, do you?"

Jane tried to shrug, weighted down by her luggage. Was she really only planning to stay for two weeks? It felt like she'd packed for a month. "Not especially. Why?"

"I've put you in the master suite." Mrs. Marshall gave an apologetic smile. "Another flight of stairs, I'm afraid. Back in the day, that's where the original bedrooms were. They've all been converted to bedrooms now." She appeared to recollect her train of thought. "The master suite was Ramsay's bedchamber, and it is said that his ghost occasionally appears there."

"Have you seen it?"

"No, but a couple of guests have mentioned it. He's utterly harmless." Mrs. Marshall bit her lip. "Do you want to change rooms?"

"No, I'm sure it's perfectly fine." Jane didn't fancy carrying her bags any further. "Ghost or no ghost."

Reaching the next floor, she looked over her shoulder at the portrait. Perhaps it was a trick of the light, but Ramsay stared straight at her. She definitely had to come back and examine him more closely.

She hurried to catch up with Mrs. Marshall who had already started on the next steep flight. "You've never considered selling that painting?"

"Oh, I've considered it a number of times," Mrs. Marshall replied, "but once I had it restored, I just couldn't part with it. It's had a turn or two at the local museum, but it belongs here in his home, don't you think?"

She murmured in agreement.

Mrs. Marshall opened a door on the third floor. "This is it. It's not all the original furniture, of course, and there are a few modern conveniences. The television is hidden in the wardrobe, and the bathroom is through that door there." She pointed to a white-painted door that looked like a closet. "There's a binder on the dresser that tells you more about the history and the items in the room. I hope you'll be comfortable during your stay. Do let me know if you need anything. Remember breakfast is at eight."

The door closed. Jane's bags fell with a muffled thud onto the thick burgundy carpet. She expelled the air from her lungs in a huge sigh of relief. She looked around at the cream-colored walls and faux Chippendale furniture. Alone at last.

Alone.

She flung herself onto the bed and gazed at the canopy overhead. Ivory cotton grown ecru colored with age was gathered in a linen sunburst at the center, the folds radiating outwards.

Alone was best. She couldn't hurt anyone that way. She had learned that lesson at long last. You could only break so many hearts. She could only break her own so many times before it wouldn't go together again anymore.

She felt weighted down on the bed, as if all her cares, all her guilt had a physical presence to pin her in place. Her leaden arms and legs had no desire to help her up, unpack, and call work to see if everything remained under control.

She rolled over, curling up into a fetal ball and started to cry.


The chill woke Jane from an uneasy sleep. Burrowing down further under the blankets, she tried to orient herself. Where was she?

She remembered the hasty trip from London's Paddington Station to Bath, her city of solace. Terrance had become far too needy and Adam wanted her back. Having two emotionally deficient men on her doorstep was too much. It was over with them, and the sooner they realized it, the better. Hopefully, escaping town would be a big enough hint for them to stay away.

What time was it? The cold hadn't dissipated. Groggy, she reached for another blanket. She fumbled for the woolen covering, trying to find the edge of it, blearily peering into the utter darkness of her room.

She frowned. Something white fluttered at the end of her bed and grew still. She didn't remember seeing anything white there before. Not that she'd paid much attention to the room.

Had the breeze from a window stirred the bed curtains? She didn't recall any of the windows being open. She blinked, clearing the sleep from her eyes.

The white form coalesced into shades of gray. The outlines grew clear. The room was pitch black, yet a light seemed to come from somewhere, allowing her to see. She held her breath.

A man knelt at the foot of her bed. His hands, clasped in a fist, concealed his face. Her eyes widened. Was he praying? Did the light come from him?

An angel or a ghost? At that moment, Jane became a believer in both.

She didn't move a muscle, watching the ghost pray. If he

had such faith, why did he remain to haunt his room? What had happened?

She inched into an upright position and leaned forward. She'd never seen a ghost before. Part of her screamed, *Get out now!* Until this moment, she'd never understood why the girls in the horror-schlock films didn't run to safety. She did now. Too much curiosity for their own good.

Having long since numbered herself among the "Too Stupid To Live" sorority, a clique she'd belonged to since her first fling with a married man, she stayed motionless, taking her fill of the ghostly figure.

He was utterly male, even in this submissive position. Tension radiated from his hunched, broad shoulders. Was it frustration or anger? She saw the crisp outline of his coat, pulled tight over his rounded, broad shoulders.

A wave curled through his hair. She hadn't noticed that in his portrait. Even though he hadn't shown his face, she knew it had to be Ramsay Chadwick. Hadn't Mrs. Marshall said he haunted the room?

The level of detail in his form fascinated her. Suddenly, he gave his head a shake. She almost screamed. She bit down hard on her lip, willing herself to silence. If she didn't move, didn't make a noise, maybe everything would be all right. Every muscle in her body howled that it was ready to run whenever she was.

His hands lowered from his face, and the fear dissipated from her in relief. No death mask, no bones, no deteriorating flesh. He looked as whole as he did in the portrait. If anything, he looked a little older. Tiny, faint lines radiated from the corners of his eyes, which were squeezed shut now.

His brow furrowed, the grim set of his mouth twisting in a brief spasm. He looked up, right into her face.

Her heart hammered, and she fought the need to scream. She could've sworn his eyes were blue. Color in an apparition was unusual, wasn't it? Maybe it was more like a black and white film where her mind supplied the colors.

One thing was for sure: he was more handsome than his portrait indicated—and that painting had been excellently done.

He stared at her. She saw all his cares wash away in shock. They both seemed frozen in place. His gaze dropped, and so did his jaw.

She glanced down at herself and saw that her skimpy nightgown revealed more than it should. She was flashing a ghost! Her breath escaped in an amused gasp. She hastily covered herself with the silken material.

When she looked up at him again, he had vanished.

She lay back, breathing hard. At least the ghost had some propriety!

Ramsay Chadwick sat back on his heels, staring at his bed. She had been so clear. She could've been a real person, sitting in his bed, if she hadn't been devoid of all color. This was the first time one of the blurred figures in his bed had seemed more substantial.

At least she had some propriety, he thought, covering herself when she realized her flimsy gown had exposed her. He rubbed at his temple. That was stranger still. Past hauntings had usually ended in a soundless scream, not a tiny gasp in reaction to his seeing more of her than he should.

Her lack of attire astonished him. What kind of woman would wear so little to bed?

He reviewed his memory of it. Narrow ribbons held up the thin material, which he guessed was silk. One of them had fallen off her shoulder, revealing an ample bosom. He dwelt on the perfection of her breast. Indeed, she could have been made of marble and not insubstantial air, a perfect Greek goddess. Especially the way her hair tumbled over her shoulders.

He swallowed. He should not be dwelling on another woman's form like that. He was engaged to Miss Lydia Devereaux, and although her recent actions troubled him, it wouldn't do to think of another woman.

Or to look at another woman that way.

The way Lydia looked at his lifelong friend, Mark Darby.

He rubbed his face. Surely he had imagined that loving, conspiratorial look. Maybe they planned an amusing diversion for him. He'd been too busy with his *pro bono* clients recently. He ought to devote more attention to his sweet, lovely Lydia.

He pushed himself off the floor. It was late. He'd sunk to his knees in desperate hope of finding a solution, and God—or the Devil—had presented him with a gorgeous succubus instead.

Ramsay Chadwick haunted Jane's dreams. Again and again, his woebegone expression, touched by grief and worry, rose before her mind. Did the matter worrying him during his haunting lead to his disappearance? In her dreams, she saw him wrestle with an unknown assailant, his sleeve being torn from his perfectly fitted coat. She saw him plunge to his death into the River Avon, his body pushed down the man-made slips until the fast-running river carried him from sight.

Most often, he stood before her, no matter which direction she turned in, holding out his arms to her, beseeching.

His spirit touched her heart. But what could she do to help?

By the time she rose and dressed for breakfast, Jane decided she'd imagined the entire thing. Nobody could see a ghost *that* real. Her imagination had taken the portrait on the stairs and Mrs. Marshall's warning of ghosts and had run with it.

She must have dreamt the whole thing. There could be no other explanation.

Downstairs in the breakfast room, she picked from the

three choices for breakfast and retrieved the paper from a high table by the door. She flicked to the financial section.

Mrs. Marshall interrupted with breakfast. Jane had chosen the healthier fruit and yogurt option. She needed to make a new start and that included taking care of herself.

"You look tired." Mrs. Marshall lingered by her table, pouring her a fresh cup of tea. "Is everything all right?"

So much for her new start. Waking up exhausted was not the way to go. The hot tea scalded Jane's lips, but she bravely swallowed. "Fine, fine."

"No ghosts?"

Jane managed a laugh. "Does dreaming about him count?"

Mrs. Marshall smiled indulgently. "No, I think not. More toast, dear?"

She shook her head. She didn't want to overdo breakfast. Even if the homemade marmalade looked awfully good.

Afterward, she let herself out of the B&B. She gazed across the green expanse of the Royal Crescent's park to the stepped rooftops of central Bath. Had Ramsay Chadwick paused on his doorstep every morning to take in this beautiful view: the golden-hued stone of the buildings, grayer now from pollution and overcast skies; the rise of green hills beyond; and the dark silhouette of the Prior Park estate?

Perhaps he just hopped into his carriage and drove off, she thought, striding along the pavement. She inhaled the crisp air. It cleared her head, and she smiled contentedly, her backpack slung over her shoulder, her umbrella swinging loosely from the other hand. It might be late summer, but rain was forecast.

She left the Crescent behind and entered a straight row of terraced houses. She planned to head straight for the center of Bath's downtown shopping district, then waste time meandering through the shops, and perhaps stop for traditional afternoon tea.

She did all that in a couple of hours, far less time than she had planned. She'd found the scones were tiny if filling, but the generous helping of jam and butter more than made up for it. She imagined they'd be even better with clotted cream. In the end, she drifted over to the Parade Gardens, situated above the River Avon but below the level of the city.

Beyond the park, the river roared with the contents of the recent rainfall, bouncing over the man-made falls and out of the city. She found an empty, damp bench and sat.

She pulled out a magazine she'd bought and tried to read it, but her gaze kept drifting from the page. From where she sat, the river was invisible, although its clamor pounded her ears. She looked over her shoulder at the stone balustrades rising above the park, softened by giant pots of pansies. Facing the river again, she gazed at the tall leafy trees and the rolling hills beyond, letting her mind empty.

Her stubborn mind drifted to her nocturnal guest. Had this park existed then? What had he done with his days? Was he a gentleman of leisure, or had he worked?

One question kept repeating: why had he disappeared?

She tossed the magazine into her backpack. While thinking of a man centuries dead was better than dwelling on her last two relationship disasters, she was here to enjoy herself, not obsess.

After another couple of hours of frustrated shopping, she decided to return to the B&B. The slog up the steep hill leading to the Circus almost killed her. Panting, she paused and did a 180, trying to stretch her aching calf muscles. This hill would take some getting used to.

She spotted a sign on a nearby post. It advertised the Jane Austen Centre. She planned to do all of the museums, and the Centre looked like a good place to start. It meant going back down the hill, however, and she was in no mood to climb it again.

For a brief moment, she imagined Ramsay Chadwick and Jane Austen meeting. A brief bow from him, her curtsy a little deeper. Jane's eyes would peep speculatively through her eye-lashes when Chadwick continued on his way.

Her lips twisted at her foolishness. They had probably never met or spoke. From what she remembered reading about Austen's time in Bath, the author didn't get out much, and yet everything she had read about the city seemed to be imbued with Austen. With that thought, Jane decided she'd take her namesake's walking tour as well tomorrow.

Turning, she noticed a flyer attached to a railing. It promoted a Beau Nash evening at the Bath Assembly Rooms on Friday.

She grinned, pleased. She'd dragged along her dancing cos-tume on the off chance the locals had something planned. There was nothing like elegant folk dancing to get her mind off mat-ters. Unfortunately, it was also how she'd met that wet Terrance, but the joy of dancing eclipsed such minor catastrophes.

The bounce returned to her step and she made it the rest of the way up the hill without mishap. She grabbed dinner at a nearby chippy and ate it on the lawn in front of the Royal Crescent. She watched the sun set, lingering until the grass became too cold and damp to endure.

She had planned a quiet night in, perhaps spent reading some of that history in her room. She dusted off the back of her jeans, disposed of her fish and chip wrapper, and returned to Chadwick's B&B.

The quick skim of the old binder Mrs. Marshall had cre-ated soon turned into a lengthy read. With a couple of milk chocolate bars as dessert, she devoured the story of Ramsay Chadwick along with the smooth, creamy chocolate.

Mrs. Marshall had gone so far as to detail the history of each historic piece of furniture in the room. The place had been gutted after Chadwick's disappearance, Jane learned, and frequently, Mrs. Marshall had had to install reproduction pieces in its place "to evoke the beauty and elegance of the

Regency period," she read aloud. Even if some of those pieces were Victorian, coming practically half a century later.

Jane glanced about the room. Well, she had to agree that the room was very pretty. Mrs. Marshall had added a nice feminine touch with lace doilies and little flower vases.

She listened to the grandfather clock downstairs faintly chime the hour. Midnight! Time to turn into a pumpkin. She slipped out from under the covers and headed into the bathroom to prepare for bed.

Once back in bed, she turned off the light and snuggled beneath the extra blankets she'd piled on the bed.

No icy ghost would disturb her tonight.


Some hours later, she woke, her face freezing. She ducked her head under the covers for all of thirty seconds before her brain started functioning. The source of that cold draft had to be the delicious Ramsay Chadwick. She'd made sure all the windows were closed before retiring.

It had to be him!

She smirked. Had she just thought a ghost was delicious? She must've had too much chocolate!

With a tentative hand, she furled down the edge of her quilt and peeked out. Her initial scan of the room revealed nothing. Maybe it was just a cold draft, left over from the rain.

Instead of rolling over and going back to sleep, she sat up, pulling a blanket around her bare shoulders. Her view had been restricted, after all. She could only see a quarter of the room when lying down. What if he were at the foot of her bed again? She had to know.

She took a deep breath and looked.

He sat on an invisible chair in the far corner of the room, right where Mrs. Marshall had chosen to place a chest of drawers. He bent forward, his head buried in his hands. She thankfully noted that his head remained attached to the rest of his body.

She wrapped her arms around her shins, resting her chin on her knees, watching him. His shoulders, although hunched, looked like they had the potential of mouth-watering broadness. He didn't move at all, his long fingers covering his face.

He had very nice hands. A heavy signet ring glowed on his right ring finger. She couldn't tear her eyes from him: he seemed so tragic and yet so strong at the same time.

Watching, she wished she could do something for him. But how could she, living almost two hundred years after he did? In any case, she didn't fancy her chances at being successful. She broke hearts, not mended them.

If only it were different.

And it would be, she vowed. No more falling into bed before falling in love. No more married men. Background checks before giving her heart. Maybe even psychoanalysis, she added to her mental to-do list, remembering the way Terrance clung to her, virtually stalking her after their breakup.

That had creeped her out so much that she'd packed her bags to come to Bath. Maybe absence would make the heart forget.

Ramsay's ghost stirred. She forgot all her problems and held her breath. He straightened, lowering his hands to his thighs. She watched his fists clench and unclench while he sat, his back ramrod straight.

His immobile face gave no hint to the emotions within him. No, she readjusted her opinion, it concealed his feelings. Only the twist of his lips displayed the bitterness, the rancor that he must feel.

His moue faded when his gaze met hers. He stared at her as if she were an exhibit at the zoo. She boldly returned his gaze, not budging. A bizarre thought crossed her mind: was he trying to will her out of existence?

Well, she wasn't going anywhere. He was the ghost, not she. She folded her arms and glared back at him.

When he stood and strode towards her, she came to the belated conclusion she'd taken the wrong attitude. You don't want to get a ghost angry.

She backed down, scooting to the far side of the bed. If he came after her, she could make a run for it to the door.

Right on the edge, ready to sprint for safety, she saw the ghost pause. The irritation on his features faded. How odd, she thought, he looked hurt that she would run away from him. He looked almost lost.

This, she reminded herself, is where the ghost turns into some hideous monster and the walls run with blood. A shiver ran through her and she pulled the blankets around her, curling against the headboard.

No more horror films for her after this, either.

The transformation didn't take place. He ran his fingers through his hair, making a second pass to smooth down the mess he'd made of it.

Jane decided she liked it messy.

He definitely looked lost, forlorn. No danger at all, right? Instead of running to the door, she slid closer to him. He stopped, an arrested expression on his face. She abandoned the blankets. Blind Freddy could see he needed comfort. Where was his fiancée?

Oh yeah. It wasn't the done thing back then to be in the same bedroom as your betrothed. Maybe it was a crazy idea, but if she could just touch him, reassure him, even if he was a long dead—

Reaching out to him, she unbalanced and slipped off the bed, landing with a thud on her behind. He vanished, one hand outstretched.

She stared at the dark space where he'd stood. Damn, she thought, even dead men run out on me. It was probably for the best. Men had to realize she was no good for them. Heck, even a ghost had figured that one out.

Who was she? Ramsay's thoughts spiraled in an ever diminishing circle around his lady ghost. Her apparition continued to be crystal-clear, but even more astonishingly, her attitude toward him was bolder than brass.

He'd almost expected to see her again tonight, and he hadn't been disappointed. She'd been more modest this time, concealing her slender shoulders and ample bosom beneath blankets.

That is, until she'd started to come towards him. The way the blankets had slipped from her, she had appeared to rise from a wave like the goddess Aphrodite.

In a dream, he'd actually started to reach out to her when she'd vanished. It was stupid and idiotic of him. As if touching her spectral form could make an ounce of difference.

Ramsay frowned. But he'd gained the impression she had wanted to reach him. Why?

He had to find out more about her. Perhaps he could lay her ghost to rest and peace. A woman that beautiful deserved it. At least he could do something about her poor soul, even if he couldn't figure out what was going on with his own life.

When Jane woke in the morning, she knew one thing for sure. She had to find out more about him. Perhaps she could lay his ghost to rest and give him peace. A guy who looked that decent and honorable deserved no less. And that cute. At least she could do something about his poor, lost soul, even if she couldn't figure out what was going on with her own life.

# Chapter Two

On the way down to breakfast, Jane paused on the stairs and gazed up at Ramsay Chadwick's portrait. Even though it showed her his fair coloring, it did not nearly do the ghost justice. How must he have looked in the flesh in full color?

"Why do you haunt me?" she whispered. She descended the last few steps to the landing and crossed to his portrait. "What can I do to put you to rest, you poor, lovely fellow?"

An ache, a longing to do something, anything, to make another happy washed through her. *Stop it,* she told herself, *you know you'll get into trouble again.*

But this time it would be different. This time her heart wouldn't be involved. It couldn't be. How could you love a dead man anyway? No matter how cute.

Downstairs in the breakfast room, she placed her napkin over her lap, smoothing the ends nervously. "Mrs. Marshall," she began, hesitant to say anything. But she had to know more about the ghost.

Mrs. Marshall, holding an empty breakfast tray, paused in the doorway. It was the middle of the week and the tourist season was almost over. Only she and Jane shared the breakfast room.

"The ghost . . ." Jane began.

"You saw him?"

Biting her lip, she nodded.

"Honestly?"

"Yes, I saw him." Seeing Mrs. Marshall's stricken face, she hastened to reassure her. "You were right; he's utterly harmless."

Mrs. Marshall managed to smile. "Now that you've seen him, he won't be back. He never makes a repeat visit to the same guest." She disappeared back to the kitchen.

Disturbed, Jane glanced down at the congealing fried egg and bacon on her plate and pushed the grilled tomato to one side. Ramsay had visited her twice now. She decided not to say anything about that. Who knew what Mrs. Marshall would do if she did, and Jane wanted Ramsay to herself a little while longer.

"Is there anywhere I can find out more about him?" She twisted in her chair as Mrs. Marshall reentered the room.

"I only know what's printed in the guidebook," her hostess replied. "Perhaps Mr. Jenkins, the fellow who wrote it, may have more information. I have his address somewhere."

She bustled out of the room and soon returned. "Here," she said, handing Jane a scrawled upon business card. "You'll find his office near the railway station."

Jane tucked the card into her jeans pocket. "Thank you. I'll let you know what I find out."

"Oh, please do. It's such a romantic, sad story. That's his fiancée there, Lydia Devereaux." Mrs. Marshall pointed to a small portrait on the wall before scooping up the teapot. "Let me get you some more tea."

Jane examined the pastel sketch of a sweet-natured, beautiful girl with blond ringlets curling about the heart-shaped face. Truly a beauty.

The phone rang in the hallway, and Mrs. Marshall went to answer it. She stuck her head around the doorway. "It's for you, dear."

Jane accepted the receiver, burying a heavy sigh. It had to be work. Something had gone wrong, and she'd have to go back and she'd never find out more about Ramsay Chadwick. "Hello?" She glanced at Mrs. Marshall hovering and managed to smile. "Patricia? Is everything all right?"

"Everything's fine," her friend and coworker's voice came down the line. "The place hasn't burnt down yet."

"That's good," she returned, twisting the phone line about her fingers. "So what's wrong?"

"Well . . ."

"Patricia . . ." Her friend's hesitation wasn't promising.

The words came out in a rush. "Terrance came in yesterday afternoon right before closing."

Jane squeezed her eyes shut at the news. He'd been haunting the street outside her shop, but this was the first time he'd dared to enter.

"You didn't tell him where I was?" She couldn't help the tiny note of panic that crept into her voice. Her holiday in Bath would be ruined if Terrance showed up, begging her to come back to him.

"*I* didn't."

Jane didn't miss the emphasis. "Who did?"

"Sarah did." Patricia sounded apologetic. "She was only trying to be helpful. You brought him to the Christmas party, remember? And no one but me knows the two of you split." Her voice took on a cheery tone. "On the plus side, she didn't tell him where in Bath you were staying."

"Great," Jane growled. "Look, can you tell everybody there that if anyone else comes looking for me, I'm in Paris?"

"Anyone else?" echoed Patricia disbelievingly. "There's someone else?"

She huffed a brief laugh. She'd been too embarrassed to let Patricia know that she'd been dating Adam as well. "Let's just say I'm trying to uncomplicate my life here."

"Okay." Patricia paused and Jane waited for the other shoe to drop. What else had gone wrong? "Jane, I know you don't want to hear this, but I dreamt about you last night."

*Oh, no. She's going to tell me it's another of her prophetic dreams.* She managed to joke, "So long as it wasn't kinky, you can dream whatever you like."

Patricia made a rude noise. "Just be careful, okay?"

"I will," Jane promised and rang off.


Unable to find anything on his ghost lady, Ramsay took refuge at his club, the dark, smoky interior an appropriate retreat from a frustrating day. He reviewed the results of his research. A woman had lived in the house before him. A number of them, actually. However, none appeared to have come to a bad end worthy of a haunting.

The nearby rub of cloth against leather distracted him from his musing behind a newspaper. He glanced around the side of it. Mark Darby sprawled in the wing chair next to his. "Evening," Ramsay said, not letting the ice thaw in his voice.

Mark raised his eyebrow. "Rough day, old man?"

He shrugged. "I cannot complain." He folded the newspaper and placed it on the cherry wood side table. He took a fortifying breath, tasting the tobacco from pipe and cigar on his tongue. "Mark, I feel I need to remind you that I am engaged to Lydia."

"Remind me?" If there was a hint of bitterness in his laugh, Ramsay was unable to detect it. "You haven't stopped reminding anyone in sight since she accepted your proposal." He paused. "Mind, you have been quiet of late. Is aught the matter?"

Ramsay rubbed his upper lip with his index finger, considering. Darby's response seemed guileless, innocent. "I have seen—looks—between you and Lydia—"

He got no further. Darby burst out laughing. A sibilant chorus of annoyed shushes rose from the adjacent chairs. He covered his mouth, subsiding into chuckles. "That's coming a bit too brown, isn't it, old boy? Lydia and I are chums, nothing more." He paused, twirling the stem of his crystal glass between two fingers and watching the claret swirl. "This must be nerves, not the green goddess of jealousy talking. How many days until the wedding is it now?"

"Less than two weeks."

"You're not having second thoughts, are you?"

"Of course not," came his clipped response. Did he hear a note of eagerness in his friend's voice? At this point, discretion seemed advisable. He had no proof other than the exchange of meaningful glances that perhaps he'd imagined after all. "My apologies for doubting you," he said with a grim, little smile. "Perhaps it is just nerves."

"You? Nervous? Then that deserves a round of drinks." Grinning as if the entire conversation hadn't bothered him, Darby raised an arm to attract a waiter's attention. "The usual do you?" Ramsay nodded, retrieving his newspaper.

He still felt ill at ease when several hours later, he stumbled up the stairs to his bedchamber. Brandy hadn't soured his head. If anything, the alcohol had made everything clearer.

He caromed off the wall and grabbed the banister to steady himself. Lydia loved him, he was sure of that. She was everything he wanted in a woman, in a wife, and more. None could compare with her beauty or her elegance.

He closed his eyes, willing Lydia's visage into his mind. He sighed. Those innocent, wide blue eyes; the clarity of her creamy skin; the way her blond hair wisped about her face like a fairy's. He snorted at his fantastical ramblings.

First ghosts and now fairies haunted his life. What next?

Just thinking of ghosts brought a mental image of her

white figure. What would she look like if she were more than white and gray?

He shook his head, giddily rocking back on his heels. Lydia. He must think of his darling Lydia. Real flesh and blood; a woman whom he could touch and who danced and sung like an angel; and with perfect manners, deportment, and modesty.

None of which, he was sure, his lady ghost was at all capable of.

Opening the door to his bedchamber, he called out to his valet. "Trenby!"

Trenby appeared in an instant. "Welcome home, sir." He helped Ramsay remove the superfine black coat, folding it over his arm.

No, Lydia was not in love with Darby; she couldn't be, despite their shared conspiratorial looks. If she did love Darby, she would not have chosen him. She loved him. Darby denied any liaison, and he had no other proof. He was imagining things.

In short order, Ramsay massacred his still perfectly tied cravat, pulling the windings from around his throat. A cool breeze tickled the exposed area.

Rubbing the back of his neck, he held out his other arm for Trenby. His valet unfastened the lace from his cuffs, shaking the sleeve fabric loose. Ramsay obligingly, if unsteadily, bent his knees, bending forward so that Trenby could heave off his shirt.

He shot upright and turned, fighting off the sudden nausea, not wanting Trenby to see it. The bed caught his eye. Something lay humped beneath the tapestried bedcovers.

He frowned, puzzled. "Trenby, what's in my bed?"

The valet peered around him. "I don't know, sir. I don't see anything."

He swallowed hard. The lump stirred and his white ghost lady's head appeared, thankfully attached to her body. He snorted. He'd heard one too many tales of headless horsemen in his youth. She stared right at him, her eyes wide.

"You don't see that?"

Trenby returned from his closet. "See what, sir?"

"That." He noticed his arm shook slightly. "Her."

"I don't see anything, sir." Trenby's cautious, skeptical voice made Ramsay realize that he was utterly foxed. Had to be. If Trenby didn't see it, then there couldn't be a ghost there. She was nothing more than a figment of his addled imagination.

"'M foxed," he muttered. "Go to bed, Trenby. I can finish undressing."

"Yes, sir."

Ramsay ignored the doubt in his valet's voice and waited until the door closed.

Then he walked toward the apparition.

Jane almost expected the cold draft before it came. She waited a moment to make sure it wasn't just a breeze and sat up.

Oh. My. God.

Ramsay Chadwick stood before her in all his half-naked splendor. She wanted to cheer. He wasn't one of those Englishmen who hid stooped shoulders and sunken, flabby chests beneath well constructed and padded clothing.

No indeed. Ramsay Chadwick was all man. The lack of color gave him the appearance of a Michaelangelo sculpture, each muscle clearly delineated. He wasn't all huge muscles either. He tended to leanness, his broad shoulders tapered to a hard, flat stomach; a whisper of hair from his belly button disappearing into his breeches. He was perfect.

She forced her jaw closed. He strode toward her, one step unsteadily following the other. He'd lost the rigidity she'd noticed earlier. He moved smoothly and without inhibition like a wild jungle animal.

She sighed. What a shame he was dead.

He reached the bed. She saw him sway, although by the grim set of his mouth, she knew he was trying to conceal it. At least part of his sexy stride was due to the consumption of liquor, she guessed.

His mouth moved, but no sound came out. She frowned, trying to understand or even to lip read, but with 20/20 hearing, she would be lucky to figure out even one word.

Not that she would stop trying. She crawled out of the bedcovers, pulling down the hem of her negligee over her thighs. His hand wiped down his face. He stopped his attempts to speak, licking his lips in apparent nervousness.

His arm waved dramatically and he started talking again. If only she could understand what he was saying. She crawled across the crumpled counterpane, her gaze fixed upon his mouth.

A very kissable mouth.

His lips thinned, becoming remarkably unkissable. He seemed upset about something. She crawled closer.

She swung her legs over the edge of the bed, reaching out to him. What was this incomprehensible magnetic pull toward him? Why did she feel the urge to soothe and comfort a dead man?

Especially as she had no luck with men living, let alone dead.

He stepped back, warding her off. When she inched forward some more, he turned and stormed away. The moment she got to her feet, he vanished.

Jane sat back on her heels, adjusting a shoulder strap. That was odd. She got the distinct impression he was upset at her. Why?

\* \* \*

Ramsay pulled a quilt from his sleepy valet's room and padded downstairs to the drawing room. Sure, he could have slept in the spare bedchamber, but it lay too close to his room and the ghostly succubus who cajoled him within.

He settled onto the sofa, feeling the cold kiss of the amber silk brocade lace on his bare back. The way she had gaped at him. Such an utterly forward creature. Perhaps he'd taken the wrong path in researching her background. More likely, she was some common maid taken to mistress and cast off to a black, miserable end, her spirit left to haunt the place of her last happiness.

Wearily, he closed his eyes. He had to stop thinking about the ghost. The way she had crawled toward him like a complete wanton, like a tigress stalking him, had set his blood afire.

Ridiculous. He loved Lydia, and he would show the whole world his love.

The idea came to him in a white flash. He would show everyone how much he loved her by holding a ball in her honor. A public shower of affection was just what they both needed. The size of his townhouse meant that it would be a small, select affair, but so much the better. Lydia would love the exclusivity of the event.

A small smile crossed his lips. Yes, indeed. Lydia would be grateful, and she would display that gratitude in a most pleasing manner. There would be no more doubts or fears. His troubles would be over.

And maybe that ghost would leave him alone.


Jane returned to Manvers Street. Mr. Jenkins hadn't been in his office yesterday. Doing field research according to the metal-encrusted teen, who sorted through piles of paper on the office carpet. She hoped to find him in today.

The small, dingy office was situated behind the bus station.

The strong, acrid odor of diesel wafted across the asphalt and into the tiny office, which shared its premises with a large bookseller. She rapped on the door and the teenager opened it.

"You're in luck," the teenager said. "He's here." He stood aside and let her in.

Mr. Jenkins, a tweed-coated gentleman in his sixties, looked up from his desk, his balding head shining in the overhead fluorescent light. Yesterday, the office had looked like a bomb had hit, and its appearance was no different today. A disposable cup of coffee balanced precariously on a low pile of paper.

"Ah, yes." He peered at her through bottle-thick glasses. "Johnny said you'd dropped by yesterday."

She cast around for somewhere to sit. All the chairs were also piled with papers, magazines, and other ephemera. "I want to find out more about Ramsay Chadwick. The ghost who haunts Chadwick's B&B? You wrote about it for Mrs. Marshall."

His lips creased in distaste. "She sent you, did she?"

"She said you would know more."

"That'd be right," he muttered. "Won't give me the time of day, and then she sends me bloody tourists." Jane pretended she hadn't heard. He pushed his glasses up his nose. "What do you want to know?"

"Anything and everything you have. For starters, the details about his fiancée's death and his own disappearance. I know he was a magistrate."

"And a Bath Councilor," Jenkins interrupted. "Had to be, to be a magistrate. He bought the right to sit on council after his father died."

Fascinating. Not. "Was there any connection between one of his cases and their tragic ends? Any police reports? Newspaper stories? I'd like primary material, if possible." She couldn't save him all these years later, but at least she'd try solving the crime and seeing justice done. With the mystery solved, perhaps Ramsay Chadwick would finally find rest.

"There were no police in Bath during that time. Just magistrates and their assistants," the historian informed her archly. "I have a journal from one of the magistrates at the time. But it is all supposition and not very pleasant at that. Your Mr. Chadwick was an unpleasant man by all accounts."

"He was?" But he looked so nice. She sighed. She should have known, of course, that there would be more to the man than his misery and good looks.

"Consorted with the riffraff of Bath, the very lowest of the low." Mr. Jenkins rose and headed for one of the battered battleship gray filing cabinets that lined the walls. "I have a facsimile of it somewhere.

"Mind you," Mr. Jenkins' voice emanated from the depths of the filing cabinet, "the magistrate didn't like Chadwick. He came from trade, you see."

"The magistrate or Ramsay Chadwick?"

"Chadwick, of course. Didn't you read that in the booklet I wrote for Mrs. Marshall?" Mr. Jenkins surfaced from the filing cabinet with a black binder. "Let me mark the passages for you." He sat at his desk and flicked through the photocopied journal. To Jane, it seemed like he stuck yellow tabs almost at random.

"Johnny!" Mr. Jenkins called without looking up. "Get out the *Bath Weekly Chronicle,* the volume that has September, 1812 in it." He glanced at her. "You can read the newspaper account of his death here or photocopy it to take with you."

"Thank you, you are very kind." At least he hadn't completely fobbed her off.

Mr. Jenkins smiled. "I am never one to discourage interest in our fair city's history." He pointed at a ratty wing-backed armchair. "Go ahead and restack those papers somewhere else. Do you know how to make tea?" Jane nodded. "Good. Johnny's awful at it."

Smiling politely at his guests and murmuring a few words here and there, Ramsay drifted across the hall to the impromptu ballroom. He'd had most of the furniture removed so that there would be room for a small quartet and the dancing.

The smile froze on his face. Lydia and Darby waltzed— *waltzed*—past him. The worst part of it all was that they were oblivious to his presence.

He'd imagined Lydia's adoring gaze settling upon him the moment he entered the room. What a fool he had been to tell her to start the dancing without him! But business had come up, and he couldn't shirk his duty.

The couple twirled and stepped about the room. Darby seemed riveted by her vivaciousness. It was like a rosebud had opened, and Darby reaped the rewards.

Ramsay's gloved hands clenched into fists, his entire body rigid. He could not make a scene and force the two apart, yet it tore at him, their betrayal. Why hadn't Darby been honest with him?

He had not ordered a waltz for the evening, yet here it was being played and danced to. It could only have been at Darby's connivance, he realized.

Which left him to watch and pretend he had granted his permission for the dance. He could not watch.

He turned on his heel and stalked from the room, sick to his stomach at the sight of Lydia waltzing with Darby. Where had it all gone wrong?

He left his party, ascending the stairs to his private domain. He groaned. How had Shakespeare put it? That roses "being once displayed, doth fall that very hour." Indeed, the sweetness had been lost.

Irritably, he pulled off his white gloves. His feet fell heavy on the stairs. He couldn't neglect his guests for too long; someone might notice, and the talk would start. He couldn't have that.

Just a moment's peace, that's all he wanted. A quiet moment to figure out how to salvage the situation.

He swung open the door of his bedchamber and stopped, his breath freezing in his lungs.

On his counterpane, his lady ghost danced. She looked like some free spirit, a naiad or dryad twirling to Nature's tune. Her arms outflung for balance, he recognized the steps of some variation of the cotillion.

He frowned. The gown she wore was definitely *a la mode* too. Not that he was any expert in fashion, but the cut seemed correct for the gowns the girls wore. She wore demure gloves that reached her elbow.

She turned. Her eyes were closed, and he felt at liberty to examine her. He stepped into the room, closing the door behind him. Nobody else should see this, this feminine apparition.

The gown suited her. The gray skirt fell straight from her generous bosom. Indeed, the bodice clung to her upper body like a second skin.

He took a steadying breath. Despite the gloves, there was nothing proper about his ghostly miss and everything to suggest that her death had to have been recent.

With graceful movements, she arced her arms, raising them above her head as she pirouetted. The skirt twirled out, rising, showing her ankles and a hint of lissome calf.

She stopped, her back to him, and stumbled a step. It seemed that her body shook with laughter. She made a half turn, facing the end of the bed, and curtsied to the empty room.

Ramsay had the surprising, most ungentlemanly urge to stand in front of her and gaze down her cleavage. What was it about this creature that made him forget all his concerns, not to mention all his manners? He should be worried about Lydia's actions, not gawking like some green schoolboy at a ghost!

He slumped into a chair by the door. He covered his face and forced himself to think of Lydia and banish the specter. What was he to do about her? Did she truly love Darby, or had his friend, knowing his doubts, merely meant to tease and provoke him? He clung to that slight straw of hope.

His hand slipped down his face, the index finger coming to rest on his chin. His gaze lifted unerringly to his dancing ghost. He would stay a few moments more and then go back down.

He wished for a glass in his hand. A bottle of brandy would soothe him and make this private show even more enjoyable. His insides glowed from the alcohol he'd already consumed. He couldn't blame it all on the liquor though. His ghost lady intoxicated him. Surely, there was nothing wrong in sharing her moment of happiness?

Besides, without that bottle of brandy, how else could he gain respite from the gnawings on his heart? He hadn't had nearly enough to drink to do it.

The ghost paused in her dancing and raised a hand to her mouth. She tugged loose the fingers on her glove, lifting it to her mouth. Her teeth bit down on the material hard enough to remove the entire glove.

He watched, mesmerized by the slow progress of the glove sliding over her elbow and down her forearm, until she flicked the glove over her shoulder.

She started removing the other one. Was she going to strip down to that inconsequential slip of silk she wore when she lay in his bed? Ramsay's heart pounded, his mouth going dry. He should get up . . . Go . . .

Her eyes opened and she stared at him. He froze, his fingertip resting on his upper lip. He felt like the worst rakehell for invading her privacy. She should be furious.

Instead, she smiled at him and curtsied, giving him—oh,

heaven!—a glimpse of the dark shadows between breasts that threatened to escape their tight restrictions.

Did she curtsy to him or to an unseen lover?

His hand lowered to his cravat, feeling a similar tightness there. He swallowed hard.

He rose and bowed in return. He looked up, still deep in his bow, to see the ghost clap like a delighted child. Her curtsy *had* been for him. A burst of unexpected pleasure swelled in his chest.

She extended her hand to him. He walked to her, lifting his arm to accept hers. Her hand was bare, and so was his—it was positively indecent.

He shouldn't do it.

And yet . . . and yet . . . Not even Lydia had ever looked so happy to see him.

She took tiny steps toward him until she teetered on the very edge of the bed. Her hand lowered to meet his.

Fingertips just inches apart, he gazed up at her. He felt like an adoring acolyte at the foot of a goddess's statue. This close, he saw that her features, while fine, were unremarkable. It didn't matter. This free, lost spirit had already captured him. Her eyes seemed to sparkle.

It was impossible he would feel anything but icy air if he touched her, but he felt compelled to try.

And yet, he hesitated, feeling more than a little foolish at thinking they could communicate or even touch.

Stretching out for him, the ghost seemed in danger of unbalancing. Without thinking, he reached up and offered steadying support.

Their hands grasped, ice becoming warm flesh, and his world turned upside down.

# Chapter Three

Jane stared at their joined hands, distrusting her senses. His warm hand gripped hers. She could *feel* it. Tiny sprigs of red hair spouted on the back of his hand. This . . . this was impossible! How could a ghost become flesh and blood?

Her gaze traversed his immaculate starched white cuff and along the length of his coat arm.

How had this happened? She tried wrapping her mind around the concept that she held his hand, a very real hand connected to a solid-looking arm and shoulder.

She swallowed a nervous laugh, the ghoulish words of "Dem Dry Bones" leaping into her mind.

His hand whipped free of hers. She missed its warmth at once. How strange. She dragged her gaze to his face, unwilling to meet the ghost's eyes.

And what eyes. They were bluer than she'd ever imagined and yet cold—the warmth hadn't reached them. Freckles stood out in fine tan drops on his pale face. She didn't remember seeing freckles in the painting, she thought rather frantically.

His jaw had dropped, but when their eyes met, her equal shock registered, and his mouth closed with a snap.

The ghost of Ramsay Chadwick took a shuddering breath—

the ghost breathed!—and stepped back. He jabbed an accusing finger at her, his expression forbidding. "Begone, succubus!"

The rich, round tones of his rather delicious baritone voice notwithstanding, Jane took offense, arms akimbo. "Excuse me?"

Only his eyes revealed his frantic search of the room. What did he look for?

In the end, he flung his hands before his face, his index fingers forming a makeshift cross. "Begone, I say!"

She sat on the bed, amused by his attempted exorcism. "I didn't think ghosts could do that," she said, her voice wobbling.

He had riveted her attention from the very first, but now she glanced away, giving the ghost time to ease his heavy, frightened breathing.

Flames leapt in the fireplace. But that was a gas heater—there was no place for a fire. Her gaze darted about the room, and she understood the ghost's fear now.

The calming beige walls had been replaced by a dark salmon rose color, the boldness brought out by the white painted cornices and chair railing.

All of Mrs. Marshall's feminine attempts at a semi-masculine room had vanished. The wardrobe holding the TV was gone, replaced by a high chest of drawers. A wing-backed chair rested in the corner by the window. All the furniture looked new and highly polished. Very masculine.

Very *not* bed and breakfast.

The bodice of her Regency gown tightened. She clutched at the neckline, trying to steady her breathing and her racing heart. She wasn't about to faint. That would freak out the ghost of—

No, he wasn't a ghost. He was real. Real flesh and blood.

"What—what happened?" she stuttered, giving herself a surreptitious pinch. She wasn't dreaming this. Somehow she'd ended up in Ramsay's own time. She was sure of it.

"You are not real," Ramsay Chadwick declared, backing off a step. "You are not here."

She giggled. She couldn't help it. Was he trying to will her out of existence?

He ran his hand through his hair, tousling the red waves. He snatched up his gloves, smoothing his hair with a practiced movement. Without any further words, he left her.

Jane blinked at the white-painted door. At least the door color hadn't changed, even if everything else had. She let out a shaky breath. He was just going to leave her like that?

She looked around for her shoes, but she had kicked them off before climbing onto the bed. They were nowhere to be found, safe in the future where she should be.

What should she do?

Faint strains of music came from the floor below. She frowned. Ramsay Chadwick hosted a party, and yet he had retreated up here in the middle of it to sulk?

She stroked the counterpane thoughtfully. It felt like silk. In the dim light, she examined it. She'd been standing on this precious embroidered silk covering?

She stood, slipping off the bed and backing away from it. Her stockinged toes slipped off the rug onto smooth, unfinished floorboards.

Should she wait for him to come back?

She caught a glimpse of herself in the mirror. Her reflection flickered from the firelight and the uneven mirror backing.

She looked like a Regency miss. She was stuck in the Regency. Why not go down and enjoy it? Surely nobody would notice her shoes were missing. Now that she was here, she could warn Ramsay Chadwick of the impending danger to his life. Maybe such an action would be sufficient to take her back to the future.

She drew her discarded gloves from her shoulder and

pulled them on, swallowing against the butterflies that threatened to burst from her stomach.

Opening the door, she looked out. Most of the light came from below, with a single sconce lit at her level. The sight of non-electric lighting kept her fascinated for a moment watching the candle flicker against the gilt reflective back of the sconce.

She tiptoed out, the patterned tile chilling her feet. At the end of the hallway, she reached a long thin landing. She looked over the banister, down the curve of the staircase to the floor below.

Some men dressed in Regency evening attire, cravats stifling their throats, stood on the lowermost steps drinking and chatting.

She stood, riveted. Each passing moment seemed more and more unreal. She jerked back, scared of being seen by them. The hum of conversation and genteel laughter floated above the violins.

She couldn't lurk up here forever . . . could she?

He'd have to come back sometime. She could tell him then. She glanced back through the arch that led to Chadwick's room, back to her safe haven. But how safe was it really? He could return, find her there, and toss her out onto the street.

No, she decided, straightening her shoulders, she had to be of use to him. There had to be a reason she'd been brought here.

Gripping the banister, she descended. Over the heads of the two gentlemen oblivious to her presence, she searched for Chadwick. She looked into the hallway. Most of the guests seemed to be in the two rooms on either side, with a few groups of people conversing in small knots. Their lowered voices and bent heads made Jane think that they were gossiping or conspiring.

Well, with no TV, what else was there to do?

No sign of Chadwick though. There was another floor below at street level. Should she look there?

She decided against it. The party seemed to be on this floor. A good host would be here with his guests. Even one who had shirked his duties once. She'd look through the rooms for him, and if he wasn't there, she'd search further.

Consoled by her rational plan, she descended the last of the stairs. Murmuring her apologies, she slipped past the two gentlemen with their brandies. She heard one of them exclaim in surprise but ignored him, intent on finding her non-ghost.

The stuffy air stank of perfume, alcohol, and warm bodies. She checked the room on the left first as it seemed to have the most people. They lined the room two or three deep, all talking and watching the handful of dancers in the small space remaining.

Lush green watered-silk wallpaper hung on the walls, the cornices painted white with a background of moss green to match. Just over the guests' heads, she saw gilt-framed paintings and large gold sconces holding thick ivory candles.

The moment she stepped into the room, Jane realized she came dangerously close to towering over many of the women. Heads turned when she slipped by them. She could almost read their minds: who was this tall stranger with no shoes?

She hoped it was that and not because she was horribly out of place. Next to the intricate and colorful fabrics and trims worn by the ladies, she looked positively plain.

Resisting the impulse to submit to her reenactment urges and grab a skirt hem to examine it, she kept moving, reaching the inner perimeter of the circle.

At once, she spotted Ramsay Chadwick. He stood on the far side of the circle, ramrod stiff, his drawn face glaring at a couple dancing.

Why did he glare so? She glanced at the dancers.

The cause was all too easy to find. Here was the reason so

few danced. They watched Chadwick watch a handsome couple twirl about the floor oblivious to all else.

The couple made a turn and she caught a glimpse of the woman's face. Lydia. She recognized her at once. Ramsay's fiancée seemed suffused with a happy glow, her gaze fastened upon her partner.

It seemed too much to hope she danced with her brother. Not when Lydia looked at him like that!

The poor fellow, Jane thought, switching her gaze to the angry, anguished form of Ramsay Chadwick. First, he has a female materialize in his bedroom and then his fiancée literally waltzes off with a dashing chap. No wonder he's so upset.

At the very least, she could stop the gossip. She edged around the circle of watchers until she reached him. He hadn't noted her arrival at all, so she laid her gloved hand on his sleeve.

His irritated glance at her froze. His mouth worked, but nothing came out. She watched his blue eyes dart about and saw his realization that her presence was noted by others. Her own ears bore witness to that, hearing the slight rising buzz of voices. She wasn't invisible.

Without shoes, she came to his shoulder. "Dance with me," she murmured. She knew this version of the German *walse* and could dance it without embarrassing him.

His breath hissed, scandalized. "What?"

She sighed, impatient. "Ramsay, I'm real. I'm not invisible, and I'm not a ghost. Get over it already." She watched his skin darken, and his lips angrily compress. "Lydia is dancing with another man. You must dance with another woman."

"You know her—" The anger slipped, replaced by a confused, lost frown. "Why?"

"Blind Freddy can see you care too much. You're attaching too much importance to their dancing. If you're not careful, you'll turn it into a scandal."

"It may be too late for that," he growled through gritted teeth, glaring again at the dancing pair.

She feared he might be right, and she already had the second thought that his dancing with an unknown woman wouldn't exactly help matters. But she had to try. "Ramsay, don't argue with me. Just dance."

"Women don't ask men to dance," he protested, his voice low. Whatever emotion he felt, he'd now managed to bury beneath a tight mask. "Who the devil are you? How do you know who I am?"

She delivered an unruffled smile, her heart pounding with sudden fear. Could she pull this off? "I'll explain as best I can, but only if you dance. You can deal with Lydia later in private."

He muttered something as he took her hand, bowing over it. Wordlessly, but impeccably correct, he led her out onto the floor. She felt the ridges and grooves of the smooth wooden floorboards beneath her feet and prayed she wouldn't slip.

His grip felt warm and secure. With a sudden certainty, she knew he wouldn't let her fall. His gaze, she saw, kept straying to the other couple.

"Eyes on me," she murmured, stepping away to turn and come back to him.

He dragged his gaze from the couple to her, unexpressed rage trapped within his eyes. He followed the steps of the dance, drawing her near.

Standing in the circle of his embrace, she almost forgot to breathe. Rivers of heat streaked through her from head to toe. She forgot the next step and slid through it into the next.

Ramsay's face had turned into a worried frown. "We should stop dancing. This is most improper." His voice sounded a little strangled.

So he felt it too. Yet he didn't bring their dance to an end. She smiled at him, deciding to pretend that the attraction didn't exist. *This was how you got into trouble last time, remember?* she told herself. "I'll be okay. No more slips, Ramsay, I promise."

"I have not given you permission to call me by my Christian name, and yet you persist in doing so." Frustration flitted across his face, quickly masked. "Who are you?"

"My name is Jane, Jane Leighton," she replied, glad her voice remained steady despite the tremors shuddering through her. *Foolish girl. This dance means nothing.*

Hoping he hadn't felt her shake, she skipped out a step and returned to him composed once more. "I'll call you Mr. Chadwick, if you'd rather."

Her response didn't seem to soothe him. "I want an explanation for—" He paused, waiting for the steps to bring them closer. "What were you doing in my room?" he whispered.

"I wouldn't mind an explanation for it either," she replied frankly, keeping her voice equally low. She had no desire to be overheard. "You were a ghost in my room. And then we touched—"

"Temptation . . . The devil," he muttered under his breath.

"It was need," she clarified, unable to stop her lips from quirking at his superstitious words. She decided not to mention how miserable he'd looked. The last thing he needed was further pricks to his ego. "I've read about you, Rams—Mr. Chadwick. You're in danger."

He stared at her, aghast. She restrained the urge to pat her head to see if she'd sprouted horns. "Danger? What danger? How do you know?"

"This is going to be difficult for you to believe." She sure found it tough. "But I'm from the future. Almost two hundred years from now, I think." She tilted her head to the side. "What year is it?"

"1812." His voice sounded constricted. "But you—you are a ghost."

She shook her head, smiling although she felt like

screaming. There were no ghosts and she was irrevocably stuck in the past. "Nope. Sorry. And as you're clearly not a ghost either, it looks like I've come back in time."

"This is insane!" he hissed through his teeth, his fair skin purpling.

Didn't she know it? She understood his panic all too well. Ghosts weren't supposed to be real, live human beings, and she wasn't supposed to be here. She could no more explain it than she could nuclear physics. "Do you have another explanation?" She glared back at him. "If so, I'd love to hear it."

"What is this danger?" he demanded instead, dodging the unexpected. She didn't blame him. "What happens to me?"

He'd forgotten to be jealous about Lydia. Good. She decided not to mince words. She only had a small amount of time to convince him. Once the dance was over, she could be dismissed, banished from the house. "You disappear."

The corner of his mouth quirked. "Like a ghost?"

So he did have a sense of humor. She shrugged, careless of how it ruined the line of her dancing form. "You've been haunting that room ever since."

He thought about this for a little while, going through the motions of the German *walse*. "Why?"

"I don't know," she replied a little too forcefully, impatient with him. "Just because I come from the future doesn't mean I have all the answers." She paused. Could she tell him the whole of it? No, not yet. He had to buy into it one step at a time.

His dark auburn brows snapped together. "Do not take that tone with me, young lady."

She refrained from making a rude noise—but only just. "I'll be nice if you'll be nice. I'm the one who's stuck here, not you."

"Stuck?" His face blanked again. She was starting to recognize it as his "I'm not panicking" expression.

Masking emotion must be second nature to him, she

thought. "I don't know how to get back to my time," she replied, her words liberally dripping with sarcasm. "Do you?"

His mouth worked. "What am I to do with you?"

The dance ended. They stood in the middle of the floor, staring at each other. He with horror, she with something akin to hope. Maybe he wouldn't cast her out onto the streets. Maybe he had listened to her. Maybe he was a real gentleman after all.

"I don't know," she admitted at last.

Lydia and her dancing partner approached. She gnawed the inside of her lip. Talking with Ramsay Chadwick was one thing: he knew her secret. These two didn't. What if she slipped and ruined everything?

"I am going to have to introduce you, Miss Leighton," Ramsay murmured *sotto voce,* slipping his hand under her elbow. "Any suggestions?"

"Distant cousin from the country visiting unexpectedly," she said from the corner of her mouth, pasting on a smile. He blinked at her, frowning. She hoped he understood her.

Lydia's dancing partner spoke first. "I see you did not waste any time," he said to Ramsay, giving her a thorough once-over. "Who is this fair creature?"

Jane thought she'd seen Ramsay Chadwick stiff, but at this moment, it looked like someone had shoved a poker up his—

He introduced her. "Mark Darby, this is Miss Jane Leighton, a . . . distant cousin of mine. Miss Leighton, Mr. Darby." She remembered to bob a curtsy while Darby kissed the air above her hand. "Pleased to meet you."

Darby's slippery grin seemed at odds with his pasty features. Unable to detect any sign of face powder, she wondered what caused his pallor. "Come for the wedding, have you?"

She returned his grin, relieved to have the excuse delivered for her. "Yes, that's it, of course. I wanted to meet the one who has captured my cousin's heart at last." She smiled at Lydia.

Ramsay finished the introductions with an expression of distaste. Was she not good enough to be introduced to his fiancée?

Lydia's gracious, cool nod hinted at the possibility. "Miss Leighton," she said through stiff lips. "When did you arrive? You were not here at dinner."

"I chose to push on to Bath instead of stopping for the night. I couldn't bear to spend another night in a strange inn." Jane kept her reply light and easy, refusing to be cowed by this icy, beautiful woman.

She knew that warmth existed in Ramsay's betrothed; she had seen her joy in dancing with Darby. Perhaps her coolness concealed shyness with strangers.

Jane returned with a probing question of her own. "Was your dance with Mr. Darby pleasant? How kind of Ra—Mr. Chadwick to let you waltz with another."

Darby laughed. "This is the city, Miss Leighton. Mr. Chadwick would not begrudge me one dance or even more, would you, old boy?" He patted Ramsay's bicep. "Where else would she be safer?"

The lines snapped tight around Ramsay's pursed mouth. "Where indeed."

It was like watching an accident happen. Any minute now, the two men would come to blows and her attempt to avert scandal for him would be all for nothing.

Lydia slipped free of Darby's arm and weaseled her way between Jane and Ramsay. "You cannot be mad at me," she cooed at her fiancé. "You know how I love to waltz and Mark was kind enough to offer in your absence."

Jane blinked, dazzled by Lydia's blinding charm. The tense moment passed.

"I say, Miss Leighton," Darby interrupted, looking down his nose at her feet. "Where are your shoes?"

A hot flush spread across her cheeks, her toes already curling in embarrassment. "They . . . uhh . . . One of them fell apart and so I—I took them off." She concealed a wince. Her excuse meant that she could only afford cheap slippers and even then that she had to wear them repeatedly.

"We will excuse you while you fetch a new pair." Lydia's smile brushed over her and scarcely seemed to warm when she directed her attention to Ramsay.

Jane shot a stricken look at him. She had no shoes to wear; they'd been left in the future. She got no help from him, his shoulders lifting in a slight, almost imperceptible shrug.

"I—I wish I could," she stuttered, her mind casting about for a reason. "I don't—do not—have another pair of dancing slippers. There's nothing else that will suit."

A silence fell over the group. With the exception of Ramsay, who merely looked embarrassed, they stared at her with a mixture of confusion and revulsion.

"Miss Leighton," Ramsay said in a kind, yet cool voice, that matched his fiancée's, "now that you have met my fiancée, perhaps you should retire for the evening. The day has been long, and I'm sure you will want your strength to shop for replacements in the morning."

He dismissed her? She drew herself up to argue but subsided. She might know how to dance a Regency waltz, but she didn't know proper Regency manners, not enough of them. Undoubtedly, she had embarrassed Ramsay and his friends.

Lydia seemed struck with surprise. "She is staying here, Mr. Chadwick?"

*My, how formal,* Jane thought, trying to still a fresh bout of nerves. Would he let her stay? But of course, where else would he expect her to retreat to?

"For the present time," Ramsay admitted with reluctance.

Heartened by his response, she murmured goodnight. She headed upstairs, noting with a deep blush how Ramsay's guests tracked her progress. No doubt the gossips wondered why a single woman climbed to his private domain.

With no room set aside for Ramsay's "cousin," she didn't know where else to go but back to his bedroom. She curled up in the wing chair by the banked fire and watched the embers glow. What was she to do? Could they make her strange story work?

Some hours later, Ramsay, stripping off his gloves, entered his bedchamber and found his ghost curled up asleep in his wing chair. Two pale, translucent stockings draped over the arm of the chair, her bare feet tucked beneath her skirts.

Closing the door with a quiet click, he watched her sleep. The vivacity and fire he'd seen in her before had faded now into a sweet vulnerability. What was he going to do with her?

He touched her shoulder. Somehow he knew Miss Leighton would want to be included in the decision.

She started awake, staring up at him with bold, wide eyes, which lightened from brown to a murky green. Hazel, the color was called. A suitable shade for this ghost who had bewitched him.

She rubbed her face. "Oh, it's you."

*Who else would it be?* He buried the uncharitable thought. "My apologies for sending you away earlier," he said, pulling up an ottoman and sitting on it. "Your story seemed too fanciful to stand up under much scrutiny."

"They say life is stranger than fiction."

Surely not this strange. He wondered at her eerie calm. Any regular young lady would have had the vapors by now, but she seemed as at ease with him here as she had downstairs, only more so. "There is a problem: I do not have any Leighton cousins."

She sniffed. "You should've said something about that before. Besides, you had the chance to come up with something else."

*When did I have a chance to do that?* When had he even had a chance to think since this creature had waltzed into his life? He grimaced, his hands clasped between his knees. "I'm afraid I wasn't thinking too well. You are—you are rather—rather disturbing."

She snorted a laugh. "Thank you."

He considered their situation. He had hoped to find her gone, but he was not that fortunate, it appeared. "I suppose you could be distantly related by marriage. But why would you have come here?"

"Perhaps because I hoped that my distant, influential cousin would help me find a job." Her brow furrowed in a way that might have been charming, had he been in the mood.

"A position?" If she was to stay, he'd have to do something with her. "I will help you with finding employment," he said. "What skills do you possess? Perhaps I can find you a place as a governess or a companion?"

She shuddered. "No, thanks. In my time, I own a jewelry shop. I know how to run a business, but I cannot expect you to set me up in something like that. Any sales position will do."

He stared at her, feeling his stomach churn. Indeed, she could be a relation with such a strong background in mercantile. Yet it was something he wanted to escape, not forge new reminders of. She needed to do something more genteel. "We shall see." He gave her a tight little smile.

"I must seem very common to you," she said in a soft, sad voice. "I only wanted to help. You looked so sad."

He flushed. *How much had she seen?* "It is almost dawn," he said. "You must be tired. I have had a room prepared for you across the hall. We will talk further in the morning."

He stood, proffering his hand. She uncoiled from the wing chair and rose, accepting his hand only as an afterthought. She had removed her gloves. Her hand felt warm in his. She was undoubtedly real.

"Thank you for your kindness," she breathed. She glanced out the window, and he followed her gaze, seeing that the sky had turned a translucent gray, a touch of gold lying to the east.

A shudder washed through him. An image flashed through his mind of kissing her hand and drawing her toward him for a more intimate kiss . . .

He should lead her from this room now and put her a safe distance from himself. This intimacy had to stop. He knew little about her, but her apparent ease with him in such close quarters was not an excuse for him to act inappropriately. She didn't appear to expect such actions from him. Indeed, what woman would from an engaged man?

"It's dawn already." He frowned. Miss Leighton seemed much paler, as if she was about to faint, the color emptying from her face. "Miss Leighton? Are you well?"

Her hand grew icy in his grasp. She should sit down before she collapsed. Whatever had brought her back to his time now seemed to wreak its vengeance, sucking the life from her.

Her mouth moved, but no sound emerged.

"Miss Leighton?" He stepped towards her, realizing too late that she'd moved forward also. He braced himself for the collision.

A chilling wave washed over him. Miss Leighton had walked right through him. He turned, seeing her ghostly form fade from sight.

Ramsay tousled his hair, his hand coming to rest at the nape of his neck. He stared at the place she had stood before she had faded from sight. She had gone then, this Miss Jane Leighton, vanishing with the dawn like a will-o'-the-wisp.

Truly, she must be a succubus . . .

He collapsed into the wing chair, his head sagging against the curved back. Turning towards the fire, he got a whiff of her scent, something strange and exotic, not like the simple perfumes most women wore.

She had said she'd come from the future. Had she gone back there for good? He closed his eyes and groaned. How was he going to explain her absence?

He inhaled the remnant of her perfume again, trying to identify the scent. That, at least, was an easier problem to solve than . . .

He leapt up from the chair. He had no business sniffing after Miss Leighton. He was affianced to the most beautiful woman in Bath!

As for explanations, if anyone asked, he'd simply say she'd run off after embarrassing him so thoroughly last night. He eyed his bed with distaste. Did she sleep in it now at some point in the future?

He checked the room thoroughly just to make sure he was alone before he started to undress. He slid beneath the cool linen sheets, flinging an arm over his face to block the dawn's light.

He had to sleep for a few hours before his meeting with the Bath Council. His ghost had delivered her message. Perhaps she would leave him be now, in peace.

# Chapter Four

Jane shivered despite dawn's first light warming the windowsill. She sank back into the wing chair, and her rear landed on the carpet. She was back in her guest room with everything back in its modern day place. Except for the bed, which remained in the same position now as then.

She scrambled to her feet, turning in search of Ramsay Chadwick. Had he been left behind then?

The insides of her gut twisted. Ramsay Chadwick in the flesh had seemed colder than as a ghost, yet something made him vulnerable, sad, and miserable. That would be Lydia.

She sighed and lay on the counterpane, a sensible cotton instead of Ramsay's silk. At least he didn't have to worry about explaining her anymore. A ghost of a grin passed her face. Except for her abrupt disappearance.

She curled up into a ball, her eyes fluttering shut. Poor Ramsay. How was he going to explain that?

"Mr. Chadwick, what you suggest is incredible!" One of the aldermen, Mr. Gilbertson, grew red about the gills, the color at odds with the sky blue walls of the council's meeting room. "Such a scheme will encourage further itinerants to clutter up our fair city. At least the Mineral Water Hospital has use for the creatures."

"The rate of crime will surely decrease if they have food in their stomachs," Ramsay argued in a cool voice, "and not only that, but employers could also be found for them—"

"I doubt that very much," Mr. Gilbertson shot back, har-rumphing. "I have read Mr. Colquhoun's *Treatise* just like you, and I find it a bunch of arrant nonsense. The next thing you'll be saying is that we need a police force."

Ramsay gave him a wry grin. "Then you know my opinion on the matter. The Bath chairmen take more part in the thieving and fencing in this city than they do to prevent it. Getting back to the issue at hand—"

The Mayor waved him to silence. "Yes, Mr. Chadwick. We thank you for presenting this to us. We have other issues we need to discuss."

Ramsay nodded, recognizing the dismissal. He bowed to the Mayor and took his seat amongst the council members. The meeting droned on and his mind wandered. The swift rejection by the Council of his plans to rehabilitate Bath's homeless bothered him little. It was a small setback, but he moved in two circles: that of Bath's council and their free tradespeople, thanks to his heritage, but also in the more rarefied circle of high society. There, he could find a patron to aid him. If only there was another Ralph Allen, he lamented silently.

He eyed the marble bust of the man who had supplied so much of the pale stone to Bath's construction. His gaze slid out the window, growing unfocused.

His thoughts dwelt on his supernatural visitor. He hadn't gotten much out of her regarding the danger to his person last night. She might be from the Devil, no matter how sweet her looks, but even so, it would be rash to ignore her warning. But from where did the danger come?

At the end of the meeting, he left the Guildhall for his impromptu court. The rejected plans slapped against his thigh as he strode up the slight incline. He made use of the front parlor of one of Bath's many taverns for his magisterial duties. He'd found that too often, the common folk of Bath were too awed to present themselves at the Guildhall or The Crescent to see him. In addition, some of his neighbors had complained about the ruffians frequenting his doorstep.

The tavern too was a more public scene. In the spirit of the Bow Street magistrates whom he admired, Ramsay allowed anyone to watch, the tavern owner making good trade out of his courtroom. Watching crime being punished was apparently thirsty work.

He slid the plans to one side of his desk, shrugging on his long black robe of office. Sitting behind the desk, which stood on a low platform, he leaned toward his clerk.

"Let them in, Mr. Allsop."

The Council of Bath might not let him build a facility for the homeless of Bath, but at least he could do something about changing the lot of the criminal element.

Alas, there were hard cases he could not help.

"Please, yer worship," begged a bedraggled woman from the makeshift dock, an upended table. "I ain't got the blunt for a turn in the iron doublet. Ye don' know how 'orrible 'tis, locked up wiv none of the ready."

Ramsay didn't want to know, but unease unsettled his stomach. "It is not meant to be a pleasant stay," he informed her, retreating behind the cool screen of his duty, "and I would rather send you to a place of reform—"

"But I had the blunt, yer worship! Some neck or nothin' young blood robbed me!"

Ramsay raised an eyebrow. "A gentleman robbing a prostitute? I find that highly unlikely." He waved at his clerk. "Next case."

"You cold-hearted bastard!" the prostitute shrieked, struggling as two guardsmen dragged her off.

Swallowing, Ramsay stilled his features into a mask of nonchalance. At least he didn't have to bind her over until the quarterly assizes. He hated the limitations of this task, especially when he could do so much more.

He fell to musing. He had eyed the country estate for his new married life, but perhaps a finer use could be made of it. Living there permanently would certainly qualify him for a chance at a Somerset county magistracy. Perhaps there, he could build his reformatory outside the city limits.

A gentleman stepped forward, wearing the sober, neat attire of a butler. "I have come to report a burglary at Lady Whipplegate's."

The crowd leaned forward, all ears. Two of the chairmen, carriers of the city's sedan chairs and the city's ad hoc policing force, were also present, and they listened with avidity along with Ramsay. "You do not seem to have come at a run," Ramsay observed.

"Her ladyship did not want me to come," he admitted, "for the item is undoubtedly irretrievably lost. I come only to inform you of the fact."

"Is her ladyship planning on posting a reward?"

"Not at this time. You see, she believes it to be taken by one of her people."

Ramsay noted the particulars as they were related and charged one of the two chairmen to discover more. "If the culprit is on her ladyship's staff, help her to uncover him."

He rubbed his brow. It was the second such minor burglary he'd heard this week. If it were one of Lady Whipplegate's servants, he'd eat his building plans.

* * *

Jane woke from her exhausted slumber some hours later. Her bleary eyes focused on the clock. She'd missed lunch.

Stretching, she reached for the guest room binder she'd left on the bedside table.

She scanned it quickly and found the history of the house unchanged. What then had been the point of her going back if Ramsay Chadwick and his bride-to-be still disappeared?

She made her way downstairs, determined to find a cafe nearby to slake her hunger. With food in her stomach, then she could plan what else to do with her day.

"Are you all right, dear?" Mrs. Marshall called, appearing from the dining room. "Big night last night?"

Jane smiled wryly. *If only Mrs. Marshall knew the half of it.* "Something like that. I'm sorry I missed breakfast."

"That's fine, dear. Nothing that won't keep."

Jane escaped into the warm Bath sunshine. Skirting the tall black railings that edged the green, she walked with purpose down the hillside from the Crescent.

She really should eat something, but hunger pangs seemed to be the last of her problems. She gnawed at her lip. She'd let Ramsay Chadwick down. She'd caused more trouble with her appearance than anything else.

Ignoring the clouds hovering on the hilly horizon, she continued walking, reentering the city of Bath from a lower level.

It just didn't seem right. Why had she been returned to the future? What was the point of time-traveling in the first place if it was for only a few measly hours? Weren't these things supposed to have a purpose?

She stopped at a small cafe near the Parades and ordered tea and a sandwich. *Get a grip, girl. You probably dreamt the whole thing.*

*But it was so vivid.*

*Too much rich food.*

*But she'd left her stockings there.*

*Bet they're under the bed.*

Miserable, she tried to reason away last night's experience, nibbling and picking at her sandwich.

The waitress left her check at the table. "You don't like it?"

"It's fine, fine," Jane reassured her. She bit deeply into the sandwich to show her appreciation, chewing the mouthful and swallowing with a smile. "It's really very good."

The waitress sniffed in disbelief and stalked off.

Jane shrugged. She had enough problems without worrying about that kind of attitude. She finished the sandwich and swallowed the last of her tea.

Walking the streets again, she ambled down a narrow alley, glancing at the small shop signs. None really caught her interest. A faint sense of unease gripped her as if her ghostly roommate walked nearby.

She glanced around, seeing nothing out of the ordinary, just the large windows of shop fronts, oddly sedate off the main shopping streets. What she needed to do was get in touch with Patricia . . .

She winced at the thought, imagining Patricia's triumphant voice explaining all the ins and outs of channeling dead people. That was not what had happened.

Was it?

She crossed the Pulteney Bridge, ignoring the crowded shops selling tatty souvenirs. The faint roar of water from the Avon, dulled by the road traffic, rushing away beneath her did little to soothe her concerns. She tried to dismiss her uneasiness, but the haunted feeling returned.

In the end, she returned to the Circus, scaling the steep hillside. Her calf muscles ached like mad by the time she reached the top. Strung out by the effort and the continuing sense of being trailed, she paused at the top of the incline, looking over her shoulder again.

No ghost, no familiar face among the crowd. Last night's adventures had driven her off the deep end.

She snorted, bending to rub at her calf ruefully. *I really should exercise more.*

An early night was what she needed. She grabbed a light dinner at a nice little restaurant on Brock Street and returned to her rooms. With a clear head tomorrow morning, she could forget about Ramsay Chadwick's troubles and focus on her own.

Ramsay wanted to sleep. He'd spent the remainder of his day hearing petty arguments in the front parlor of the tavern. Sometimes, he wished he had the power and influence of Solomon. At least with the last case of the day, he'd been able to do something constructive.

A boy had been brought before him. He had been caught picking an elderly gentleman's pocket by one of the chairmen.

"Please, mister," the boy had begged. "I'm guilty of the crime, but I've two brothers to feed. I 'ad to do something!"

"What about your parents?"

"Dead, sir, or good as."

Ramsay pretended to consult his notes, trying to gauge the boy's personality. He sensed the boy's honesty. Many a young rapscallion had delivered similar Banbury tales with more conviction yet were unconvincing. "Very well. As this is your first offense before this court, I will go lightly."

He offered the boy a job in his stables and agreed to let his younger brothers room with him, provided the boy presented himself with his two unseen siblings that evening.

Grinning, the boy agreed. Released, he ran from the tavern.

"That's the last you'll see of him," his clerk remarked.

"If the boy refuses the opportunity," Ramsay had murmured to his clerk, "and commits another crime, chances are that I will indeed see him again."

Ramsay smiled at the memory of his clerk's cynicism. The boy, Billy, and his two younger brothers, one a toddler, had turned up on his doorstep a few moments ago.

Their arrival had made him late for the Devereaux's dinner party. Lydia would not be happy. Once dressed, he dismissed his valet.

He gazed into his shaving-glass, giving his cravat a tweak. He blinked, then blinked again.

Not again.

The ghostly apparition of Miss Jane Leighton lay in his bed.

He closed his eyes. He waited a full minute before reopening them. She hadn't done him the courtesy of disappearing. She seemed . . . asleep.

Abandoning her reflection in the glass, he crossed to his bed. The counterpane remained smooth and tight over the bed's surface. No dent or lump marked Miss Leighton's presence. His hand gripping the bedpost, he watched her sleep.

It seemed indecent, unnatural, that he should observe her at this vulnerable moment. Frown lines marred her marble-white forehead and the corners of her mouth. *What troubled her? Is that why they had made a connection?*

He *could* touch her, bring her into his time and find out, but how could he pry into her troubles unasked? Besides, what could he do to help, so far in her past?

He gazed at her white form, shaded with gray. He imagined the colors of her in life: the rich chestnut of her hair, the warmth of her hazel eyes, the rosy flush of her cheeks in anger or embarrassment. All these things he remembered from the previous evening.

He gave himself a little shake. He gazed at her like a lovesick calf. How ridiculous! It's not as if he fancied her. No, it merely fascinated him that she continued to appear in his bed.

If he touched her this time, would she wake and be in his time . . . or would he be transported to hers?

He stepped back. He couldn't stand here all night. He had his fiancée's dinner to attend.

Jane woke to darkness, a heaviness weighing upon her, the vestiges of a bad dream. Where was she? She blinked, the red glow from the alarm clock coming into focus. It was after midnight. The cold glow of a street lamp shone in through a crack in the curtains.

She sighed. Her sleep cycle was surely beyond hope now.

Closing her eyes, she rolled over and tried to sleep, but the option of slumber was denied her. She squeezed her eyes shut, willing herself to unconsciousness.

All to no avail.

She opened her eyes. Inches away, Ramsay Chadwick stared back at her.

She scrambled back, her heart thudding with shock. He lay next to her, his head pillowed by an arm, watching her. His eyes widened in alarm, tracked her progress.

Almost falling out of bed, she grabbed his shoulder. His warmth blossomed beneath her hand.

"It happened again." She gasped, struggling for breath. Although she lay beneath the covers and he on top of them in full evening dress, missing only his cravat, it was too close for her.

She didn't dare move. Breathing became difficult.

Without the cravat, he seemed so much more accessible. The open neck of his shirt revealed the strong column of his pale throat. She lifted her gaze to his face and sought to regain her internal balance.

"So I see," he said dryly. He remained motionless as well, a tense wariness about his bright blue eyes. He gazed keenly upon her face, searching it as if evaluating her.

She cleared her throat, breaking the awkward silence. "I didn't think this would happen again."

"Nor did I."

"I don't understand why this happens . . ." Clad in only her chemise, she felt grateful for the bedclothes over her. She tugged them a little higher.

"You touched me."

She snorted, dispelling the delicious shiver his soft murmur aroused. "You touched me."

"I do not wish to call you a liar, Miss Leighton, but this time, you definitely touched me. Last night, I will concede it could have been either one of us." His cool pronouncement dashed the lightheartedness she'd tried to inject into the situation.

She remembered she was not here to tease him. "Very well then, I will be serious. I have told you already that you are in danger."

A sole raised eyebrow. "If you were anyone else, Miss Leighton, I would think you were hysterical."

She matched his raised eyebrow with one of her own. "Hardly. I take it my unusual arrivals make you more inclined to believe me?"

He gave a curt nod. "I cannot think beyond that what your purpose might be, however. How can you prevent my strange disappearance?"

So he had remembered. She shrugged, the thin strap of her chemise slipping off her shoulder. "I have not learned enough about it to say, but it involves Lydia."

"I think it would be wise to keep my fiancée out of this." His frown deepened, his mask ratcheting into place.

"I have a gut feeling, an instinct," she amended, seeing his confusion at her phrase, "that she is right in the middle of it." She gnawed at her lip, thinking. "She has not wanted to cry off from the engagement, has she?"

He bolted upright, catapulting himself from the bed and

putting distance between them. "She eagerly anticipates our nuptials."

Jane sat up, pulling the covers up to her neck. From this ludicrous position—when had she become such a prude?—she asked, "Are those your feelings on the matter or hers?"

He faced her, glaring. "She is the most beautiful woman in Bath! No, England! What man wouldn't be proud to wed her?"

"Present company excepted, of course," Jane muttered under her breath.

He snorted, giving every indication he'd heard her little commentary. "She talks of the wedding frequently and of what we shall do together afterward."

*Too much information!* Jane clapped her hands over her ears, laughing. "I'm not sure I want to hear this!"

He flushed iron red, his skin almost matching the color of his hair. "I meant," he got out between gritted teeth, "that she plans to redecorate the townhouse and renovate my country estate."

Jane continued to muffle her bursts of laughter.

He pointed at her chest. "Miss Leighton, please cover yourself."

Her chuckles faded and she pulled the covers up over her nightgown. She pursed her lips. If he were so offended by her state of semi-undress, why hadn't he looked away? And what had he seen while she slept? Typical man.

"I cannot see why my fiancée would be involved, nor what you can do if you dwell in my house only between the hours of dusk and dawn."

"Lydia is very much involved," Jane argued. "She disappears too."

"What?" Ramsay bellowed. He streaked across the room and gripped her shoulders, shaking her. "Explain yourself. What do you mean, she disappears too? Why didn't you tell me this before?"

She laid her hands on his forearms, pressing down to stop him from shaking her. She fought to keep her voice steady. The sudden violence of his actions had unsettled her. "Both of you disappear without a trace. I can help. There are plenty of evening engagements and events where I can mingle and find out what's going on."

"She disappears?" His face crumpled. He looked so lost, so helpless. He must really love her, for all his talk about her beauty.

She leaned forward and brushed his cheek with her hand, wishing for some of that softness for herself. "I will help you, Ramsay," she promised. "I will see you and Lydia safely and happily wed."

His mouth tightened and he drew her hand downwards, away from his face. "That is not proper, Miss Leighton," he muttered.

"No less proper than being in your bed," she reminded him *sotto voce*. "I am not angling after you, Mr. Chadwick." *Just the kind of love you have for Lydia. Not you.* "Things are a little more free and easy in the future than here, that is all." *Yeah, like you touch all the guys like that.* "I have sworn to help you, and I will."

She reclined, putting a touch more space between them. Ramsay sat upright, his back straight. Jane sighed. This was going to be difficult. With her touch, she had broken some barrier, and he'd armed himself against that. She saw it in his emotionless face. She'd have to regain his trust now, all because of a single foolish action.

She sat up, businesslike. "Now, tell me what you have planned for the rest of the week. I shall see about getting some clothes that will suit . . ."

"I am sure I can procure something for my distant country cousin." Ramsay managed a tight smile. He looked as though he had swallowed something vile. "Who fled town but who has apparently come back again."

"That was your excuse before, eh?" She laughed softly.

He remained unamused. "And what reason do I give when Lydia and her mother want to pay you a morning visit?"

She shrugged. She doubted that Lydia would want to pursue the acquaintance of a poor cousin. She'd read enough Thackery and Austen to know that. "Tell them I am suffering the most oppressive headache, or that I am out exploring or some such thing. We will get around it."

"We will?" he asked in that cold, ironic voice she had started to despise.

She couldn't resist jabbing back, affecting his airs. "As you would say, Mr. Chadwick, most assuredly we will."

# Chapter Five

With Jane unable to return to her own time until dawn, she wrapped herself in Ramsay's silk counterpane and perched on the end of his bed, Ramsay retreating to his wing chair by the fireplace.

Decorum restored, Ramsay gave her a crash course in Regency etiquette. He seemed pleased she had the basics down already and he drilled her in the art of conversation, making sure she would not embarrass him again in that area.

Before the morning light took her away from him, he gave his nod of approval. "Very good, Miss Leighton. You have improved."

"Am I fit for society?"

"Almost."

She stuck her tongue out at him.

His brow furrowed. "You prove my point. You must temper your high-spirited proclivities, Miss Leighton, if you are to move in the upper echelons of Bath society."

"But we are not in the upper echelons; we are in private."

He colored, his light freckles sinking beneath the red tide. "That is another matter. You cannot stay in my bedroom, Miss Leighton, between the hours of dusk and dawn. The servants will gossip. On the morrow, I will have a bedchamber made up for you."

On the face of it, she found little wrong with his suggestion. Until she remembered the dawn. She grimaced. "If that happens, I will appear in somebody else's bedroom in the morning. They will get such a shock!"

His mouth twitched. "I am sure you'll think of something."

This was more than making up excuses for an absent person. "No. Unlocking a door is too noisy and I would be thrown out of the B&B—"

"The bee and what?"

"Bed and breakfast." Jane winced, anticipating his outrage. "That is what your residence is now, or in the future. A sort of hotel."

"Sort of hotel?" Ramsay looked as if he'd swallowed something unpleasant. "In the Crescent?"

"It's not the only one. Times have changed, and these old places are much too expensive for most individuals to own. Staying in a bed and breakfast gives one the chance to live such a life. There are only a few houses on the Crescent that aren't broken up into apartments."

"I see."

She suspected he didn't, but she didn't push the issue. "Can I not sleep here and you sleep in another room?"

His eyes widened. "But this is the best bedroom!"

"And shouldn't the best bedroom be offered to your guest?" she retorted with a smile. His lips pursed. "If I am asked to leave the B&B, I won't be able to come back and help you save Lydia."

He raised a single eyebrow. "Now that I know of the danger, I can save her."

Typical man, thinking he could do it alone, when he'd been blind to the danger until she'd pointed it out to him. "You're willing to take that chance?"

He stared at her long and hard. He wasn't looking *at* her, it was more as if he was evaluating the possibilities, the various paths to take. "No," he said at last. "I cannot take that chance. It would help to have an ally."

"Done." She reached out to shake his hand.

He gazed at it, puzzled.

"Shake it," she advised him. "We made a deal."

"We did?" He seemed rather befuddled.

"I get the bedroom, and you get me—to help you save Lydia."

His lips twisted in amusement. "That was the deal?" His hand clasped hers, warm and strong. "Ladies do not shake hands, by the way."

"I know, but this is—"

"—in private," he finished for her. "That will be your downfall one day, Miss Leighton. You must have a care."

"I will, I promise." She glanced towards the window. The sky was lightening. She could make out the hills beyond the city. "It will be dawn soon." She didn't really want to go.

Ramsay dashed over to a small writing desk and snatched up a quill. "Your measurements before you go. I'll see what I can arrange regarding clothing for you tomorrow."

She clutched the blanket about her shoulders, suddenly self-conscious. "Height is five feet, ten inches. Ahh . . ." She blushed, noting he had colored too. "Bust, 44 inches; waist, 36 inches—that's my natural waist, by the way—hips, 42 inches."

She watched him fade into white as he furiously scribbled down the numbers. "I'll see you tomorrow," she said and raised a hand in farewell.


Jane decided against sleep, instead staying up to review the contents of her wardrobe. She'd brought just one Regency dress with her and had nothing else even remotely Regency or Empire style. Could she make a run to London and back to pick up the rest of her costumes?

What if she ran into Terrance? She swallowed and considered her other options.

Surely she could get what she wanted here in Bath. Chewing her lip, she made a list of things she'd need. It would take ages for a custom-made gown, and she didn't have that luxury of time; however, she could purchase ribbons for her hair, stockings *and* possibly even find an evening reticule. This was Bath, after all!

She descended to breakfast a few hours later, list in hand.

Mrs. Marshall smiled at her. "Good morning, Jane. Did you sleep well?"

"For a little while," Jane confessed.

"The ghost?" Mrs. Marshall placed a fresh rack of toast on the table before her.

Jane decided to come clean. "Yes, as a matter of fact."

"How unusual. He never comes back to a guest." Mrs. Marshall frowned. "The offer is still good, my dear. I can move you to another room."

"Oh no!" Jane hastily interrupted. "I wouldn't dream of moving! He does no harm. He doesn't even seem to know I'm there." She crossed her fingers against the small lie. "It's fascinating just to watch him." That was true at least.

"If you're sure . . ." Mrs. Marshall briefly disappeared into the kitchen.

"I'm sure." Jane pasted a smile on her face. "Perhaps you can help me, Mrs. Marshall? I belong to a Regency dancing group, as you know. Is there anywhere in Bath where one might purchase material or even gowns? Perhaps a shawl? I would like to take back something new." She had one shawl already; another one wouldn't hurt.

"Let me get you the yellow pages." She bustled away and returned. "Does it have to be authentic? I noticed there were some nice bridesmaid dresses in town that had a Regency look."

Jane considered it. If the fabrics were not too modern, ditto the colors, she could possibly modify it herself. She added a sewing kit to her list. "That could work in a pinch."

Mrs. Marshall beamed. "I'll leave you to it then. Did you want bacon or sausage with your breakfast today?"

Jane flipped through the hefty yellow pages as she ate, choosing the town center shops first. If she got really desperate, she could catch a taxi to some of the outlying places.

Hours later, she returned laden with plastic and paper shopping bags. She'd put in a commission for a custom-made gown, just in case, and had found a few dresses that, with a wide ribband tied under her bosom, would fit perfectly. A few shawls and some evening gloves completed the haul.

At least today, not once had she had the sense of someone following her. Her fear Terrance had found her seemed rather irrational.

Mrs. Marshall peeked in as Jane flung one bag after the other through the door. "Your shopping a success, dear?"

"Completely!" Jane grinned back. Her credit card statement wouldn't thank her later, but right now she felt triumphant. Whatever Ramsay Chadwick and his valet came up with, at least she had found items that suited her.


One long afternoon nap and a refreshing shower later, Jane sat cross-legged on the bed, dressed in a new Regency-style gown and ready for an evening in another time.

She twiddled with the long mauve ribbons that fell from the high waistband. Would he show up or had he had second thoughts? Or maybe this time, the portal thing wouldn't work. The ribbon wrapped around her forefinger and fell loose again.

Dusk became night. Jane hadn't turned on any lights, so

she had only the glow of the alarm clock to go by. She wanted to catch the first glimmer of Ramsay's appearance.

His white silhouette moved through the closed door, his arm held out diagonally from his arm, holding an unseen doorknob. He approached the bed, his image growing clearer with the deepening darkness.

He held out his hand, and she reached to take it. She held her breath, watching his ghost-white skin ripple under her touch, warming to still pale, but real, flesh.

Ramsay appeared to have adapted to the change too. "Why are you sitting like a Red Indian?" He released her hand.

She unfolded her legs and swung off the bed. "Because it's comfortable." She twirled. "Do I pass inspection?"

He pointed to her wrist. "Except for that."

She glanced down and saw he pointed at her watch. Taking it off, she placed it on the bedside table. "Don't let me forget it."

He passed behind her and picked it up. "It tells the time? How is it so small?" He held it up to his ear. "It doesn't tick!"

"It's something called a quartz movement. Modern technology is a wonderful thing."

He put the watch back down. "Indeed," he said, trying to sound unimpressed but failing. "Shall we go? You are wearing shoes this time?"

Jane laughed. "La, Mr. Chadwick, but I do believe you are teasing me!"

His features shuttered. Had she been too gauche? "Not at all, Miss Leighton."

"Where are we going?" she asked, following him out.

"To the New Rooms."


Although the Upper Assembly Rooms were only a few blocks away along a level road, they traveled in a carriage.

"We're not walking?" Jane asked, seeing the carriage.

Ramsay looked affronted. "Of course not. That would be most irregular."

Raising her eyebrows, Jane allowed Ramsay's coachman to help her into the carriage in question. With her long skirts, it was not easy. She hiked them high, almost to the knee, in order to get aboard.

She heard a muffled oath behind her. Sitting on the soft leather seat, she twitched her skirt back into place. "My dancing lessons didn't cover carriages."

Ramsay lifted his gaze from her slippers. Was he still imagining the stockinged glimpse he had caught there? Typical.

The horses moved forward, and she gripped the dangling leather loop to steady herself. Once she had gotten used to the jerking motion, she decided to remind him of his obligations.

"Will Lydia be there?" she asked, glancing sidelong at him, his visage barely visible in the dim light.

His eyebrows rose. "Of course."

With a brief lurch, the carriage halted. Ramsay helped her descend from his carriage, and this time, she tried to keep her skirts at a discreet level. He tucked her arm into his and they strolled into the building. Ramsay handed his tickets to the doorman.

Could she carry this off? She knew the risk Ramsay ran in bringing her out in public. Her 'country cousin' excuse could only carry her so far. Her nervous smile vanished once they passed the gatekeeper, a wall of sound and smells hitting her. She paused, gasping.

This was so unlike the quiet of the costume museum. She let Ramsay lead her through the marbled columns and into the crowded octagon room, the yellow walls rendered golden by the candlelight.

Ramsay looked down at her. "Are you well?"

She flipped open her fan to get the air circulating. "Dazzled. I've never—never seen it like this before . . ." The crystal chandeliers glittered with candlelight, reflecting off the shiny jewels and fabric of the women who mingled in the dancing hall.

"Come, we need you to sign the book."

Jane knew the book he meant. She remembered Catherine Moreland having to sign it in Jane Austen's *Northanger Abbey*. It signified her official entrée into Bath society. Despite her mysterious background, with Ramsay Chadwick's support, she should have no trouble being accepted by Society.

Unless she did something very stupid.

She drank in the sights as they passed through the octagon room and into the tea room, eyeing the more fashionable gowns with envy and wishing her simple cotton white and mauve gown had more trim to it as seemed to be the fashion. A few more ruffles, and she would be *la mode*.

"Stop staring," Ramsay murmured from the corner of his mouth. "What are the Uppers like in your time?"

She appreciated him offering her the distraction and gave him a grateful smile. "They were bombed in the Second World War—" She chose to ignore his startled expression. Now was not the time for a history lesson. "They have been restored. It's a museum of fashion and costume now." She snuck a glance at a particularly stunning velvet evening gown of moss green edged in a matching satin ribbon. "They'd kill to get their hands on some of these gowns."

"Mm-hm." He steered her to the pedestal.

She tried not to stare, but she couldn't help it. There was so much to see. She longed for a notebook to scribble down her observations. They would be so valuable in the future to her reenactment group. She drank it all in, trying to memorize every moment so she could write it down in the morning.

"It's wonderful to see these rooms so full of life," she chattered in an effort to conceal her rubbernecking. "They've been left empty, and even when they have the dancing exhibitions, it feels a little melancholy."

At his direction, she curtsied to the incumbent Master of Ceremonies and exchanged a few light words with the august gentleman before inscribing her name and Bath address. She stripped off a glove to write. She struggled with the inky quill, scratching her way across the parchment.

She concealed her inky fingers beneath her white satin glove, glancing at Ramsay in time to see him conceal a long-suffering expression. "Shall we go find Lydia?"

They left the subscription book and pedestal and strolled around the perimeter of the room. Ramsay moved with a purpose: he must have been aware of Lydia's presence the moment they entered the room. Of course. She was his fiancée. The woman he loved.

They stopped before Lydia and another woman. Lydia was an absolute picture in a spotted white muslin gown, a pale peach ribbon tied under her high waist, the ends trailing down her back. He bowed and gestured to Jane. "Miss Devereaux, you remember my cousin Miss Leighton?"

Lydia's pretty brow furrowed. "Of course." She nodded at Jane. "I thought you had left Bath?"

"I had," Jane confessed, "but I came back, as you see." She spoke as if her departure and return hadn't been extraordinary.

Ramsay introduced Jane to Lydia's mother, a rotund woman in unassuming blue with a gauze scarf about her neck, before bowing again. "If you will excuse me, ladies, there is a gentleman I must speak with." He gazed at Lydia with longing. "You will dance the waltz with me?"

"Of course." Lydia's smile seemed forced.

Frankly, Jane couldn't blame her. Did Regency men not possess good manners? What had happened to 'please'? As soon as Ramsay was out of sight, she hid her mouth behind her fan and gave quiet voice to her concern. "Good grief, when did cousin Ramsay become so arrogant?"

Lydia sighed, her fan moving at a languid rate. "He has always been like that."

She'd observed his air of entitlement but he had not been *that* arrogant with her. It shocked her into asking, "Even when he wooed you?"

A gentleman approached, interrupting their conversation. "Miss Lydia, you look absolutely charming this evening. Would it be too much to hope you will reserve a dance for me?"

Lydia consulted the bones of her fan. "The third dance this evening, Mr. Wetherby?"

Mr. Wetherby clapped his hand to his breast. "I am the most fortunate of men! Allow me to take you into supper?"

Lydia smiled and flirted back. "Mr. Wetherby, you presume too much! I am an engaged woman!"

He bowed, sobered under Mrs. Devereaux's glare. "I had forgotten in the presence of such luminous beauty. Until the third dance, Miss Devereaux."

A stream of gentlemen approached Lydia after that, flirted with her, begged dances, and moved on.

Jane murmured her amazement. "My cousin does not mind all this attention you receive?"

Lydia smiled. "Not at all. He is proud to have won the most desirable woman in Bath."

Modesty did not seem to be one of Lydia's faults. "How *did* he win you? Is his aloofness the secret?"

Lydia laughed. "Gracious, no. He mooned over me as badly as all these other boys." She smiled. "I am sure there is no need to tell you how he won me."

"Indulge me." Jane's smile went razor-thin. Lydia reminded her of the most popular girl in her high school class, flaunting her popularity in everyone's faces.

Lydia's fan fluttered carelessly. "He is a rich man—and he's not hideous and elderly." Her smile grew as sharp as Jane's own. "Excuse me, I believe I am claimed for this dance."

Not by Ramsay Chadwick, who had requested only one dance, but by Mark Darby, who proceeded to dance twice with Lydia before taking her to supper. Leaving Jane with Mrs. Devereaux.

"Poor dear." Mrs. Devereaux patted her arm. They had followed Lydia and Darby into the celadon green ballroom. "Mr. Chadwick should have danced with you, and then there would be no shortage of young men wishing your company. If we could but attract his attention."

"It does not matter, Mrs. Devereaux. I am happy to observe this evening. This is far more than I ever dreamed of." She meant it. Traveling back in time was not an everyday occurrence, after all.

"You are very kind to stand with me." Jane had noticed Ramsay looking her way before, as if to ensure she wasn't standing on her head or otherwise making a fool of herself. Most of his attention, though, fell upon Lydia's dancing form. He was a jealous man, Jane decided, and he didn't know what to do about it.

"Nonsense! I cannot leave you without your chaperone . . ."

Jane smothered a grimace. She wanted to mix with the crowd and find out what people really thought of Ramsay Chadwick, hoping to discover some kind of enmity, a clue that someone in the fashionable circles was out to get him.

It was not to be, however, for Mrs. Devereaux had made it clear she was not to wander off on her own, and anyone who came to see the older woman would, of course, have nothing to say against her daughter's fiancé. "Forgive me for asking, my dear, but you do have a chaperone staying with you at Mr. Chadwick's?"

Jane widened her eyes, silently cursing. Why hadn't she thought of that? "Of course!" She smiled prettily. "I do apologize for forcing this upon you. Miss, uh, Dovetail is not well tonight. Our recent adventures have quite exhausted her. She used to be my governess and is getting on in years, you see."

Mrs. Devereaux smiled, relieved. "I am glad you have a chaperone, my dear. I am sure it is no different in the country as it is here in town. It would not do to stay alone with Mr. Chadwick, cousin or not."

"Of course, Mrs. Devereaux; the very idea is shocking." Jane repressed a rueful smile with difficulty. If she'd taken Mrs. Devereaux's advice, then perhaps she could've avoided a few disastrous relationships.

She paid attention to Mrs. Devereaux's speech again. "Any cousin of Mr. Chadwick's is welcome in our house. You must visit us tomorrow morning. If Mr. Chadwick is incapable, then I will get you settled, my dear."

Jane's smile wore thin. "You are too kind." Visiting the Devereauxs's during daylight hours was impossible, but she couldn't say that without a good excuse, and she had run out of them for the night.

She sighed. She had wanted to talk with Lydia tonight and find out what made her tick so she could help Ramsay, but the girl seemed happiest dancing with men to whom she was not engaged. She feared that she had already plumbed the depths of the girl.

The problem appeared to be Ramsay's arrogance, but she'd seen the vulnerability beneath. How could she get him to soften that hard shelled exterior and show Lydia a man she could love?

Ramsay came to rescue her after supper. "I have not seen you dancing," he remarked after greeting Mrs. Devereaux.

Mrs. Devereaux slapped his wrist with her fan. "La, my boy, but you abandoned her. If you dance with your cousin now, perhaps it won't be too late."

"How remiss of me." Ramsay's tone seemed to indicate anything but. "Miss Leighton?"

She knew the dance steps of this country dance and so took his arm without fear. That her stomach seemed packed with butterflies was due to dancing before natural experts, not to Ramsay claiming her hand. He was just a handsome guy, she thought, nothing more. She should try and think of him as her big brother, uninterested in her and of no interest to her.

They joined the bottom of the dance line, moving through the formation twice before Ramsay spoke. "You move well."

"Thank you," she returned. "Nineteenth-century dancing is a hobby of mine."

"Fortunate."

She grinned, relieved that she hadn't stuck out like a sore thumb after all. "I think so."

His expression remained unchanged. "Have you made any progress with, er, your investigation?"

She chuckled at his delicate phrasing. "Now you sound like the magistrate you are!" Her smile vanished at his even look. Did the man not possess a sense of humor? "I have not achieved as much as I would like, but this is not the place to discuss it."

The dance drew them apart long enough for her to banish flippancy and put on her professional business guise. The dance drew them back together again. "Why not?" he asked.

"Rams—Mr. Chadwick, I am a straightforward speaker. I worry you might overreact when you hear what I have to say."

He looked down his nose at her. "Then it shall indeed wait until we are in the carriage."

That ended the conversation. Soon after, the dance ended. He returned her to Mrs. Devereaux, escorting Lydia onto the floor for their waltz.

Jane watched them, aware of a faint tinge of jealousy. A handsome couple, they moved with surety and grace. She half-wished a man would look at her the way Ramsay gazed upon his bride-to-be: with such loving, hungry intensity.

The green flash faded. Her goal here was to help, not drool. She observed them: he and Lydia remained silent. He had talked, albeit briefly, with her; why did he not speak to Lydia?

Lydia's face showed no pleasure, a polite smile laid over smooth features. Jane thought she caught a flash of disdain. But had she imagined that?

*Oh dear. Those two are in trouble.*

Ramsay returned with Lydia, bowing and kissing the air over Lydia's hand. With increasing dismay, Jane saw Lydia ignore his gallantry. *What was her problem?* She held her tongue, not ready to leap in yet. She needed more facts. It might be that Lydia felt unwell this evening.

Jane sighed. But the girl had flirted with other men . . .

Another gentleman claimed Lydia, and Jane watched her transform into a laughing flirt, dispelling any chance of Lydia being ill. She darted a concerned glance at Ramsay. He didn't look happy at all.

Was their strained relationship the reason for their disappearance and demise?

He caught her looking. "You must be tired, Miss Leighton. Shall we retire for the evening?"

"I think that is a good idea." The sooner she made her observations, the sooner Ramsay could start fixing his failing relationship. Jane curtseyed to Mrs. Devereaux. "It was a pleasure meeting you. Please pass on my farewells to Miss Devereaux."

Ramsay escorted her from the assembly rooms and assisted her into the carriage. They had barely gotten underway when he began his interrogation. "Well? What did you find out?"

"I don't have enough to tell you yet." She stalled but even through the gloom, she saw Ramsay wasn't pleased with her response. "She danced with half the men in Bath, all young and good-looking, and with you only once."

"It is not the custom to dance exclusively with one man, even if you are engaged, and Lydia loves to dance." Ramsay refuted her argument.

"Have the two of you argued?" Ramsay was dreaming if he thought all was well between them. She had to show him otherwise, even if it meant facing his displeasure.

"No, of course not. We are on the most amicable terms. She is excited about her approaching wedding day, I assure you."

"So you've said." Jane gnawed the corner of her lip. She had little more than instinct on her side. It was too soon to let him have it with both barrels, not when her arguments to date had shown her ignorance of acceptable customs.

They arrived at Chadwick's house and their conversation ceased until they reached his study. At Jane's best guess, this placed her in the breakfast room if she were in the future. It seemed a shame that the light blue walls had been painted over in white. The room rather reminded her of a Wedgwood plate, the dark mahogany furniture giving it the proper touch of masculinity.

She needed more information about Ramsay and Lydia's relationship. "You didn't talk while you waltzed. Why is that?"

Ramsay turned from stoking the fire. "We do not need to talk. We were enjoying the pleasure of each other's company."

She believed that was Ramsay's motivation, but Lydia's? She was not so sure. "I think you need to keep wooing her, flattering her. She revels in the attention she gets from the other gentlemen—and she's not getting it from you anymore."

"Miss Leighton, you presume too much!" Ramsay's fist slammed down onto the sideboard. The books rattled. She jumped. Had she touched a sore spot? "Lydia knows how I feel about her!"

Jane settled into a comfortable leather wing chair, forcing her nerves to uncoil. Here was her chance to set a man straight. A man that, for once, she wasn't involved with. She spoke with cool patience. "Mr. Chadwick, a woman likes to be told often and frequently that she is loved. She likes to be shown that she is loved. If you think for a minute that putting a ring on her finger stops that need, you are greatly mistaken."

"Do not read me a lecture, miss!" Ramsay thundered, his fair skin reddening. "You are to find out why she disappears, not meddle with our love affair!"

Jane barked a brief laugh. "Is that what you call it?" she sneered, wondering if she could be any more cynical. "Ramsay, your 'love affair' is in trouble, and I'm willing to bet it is somehow connected with Lydia's disappearance."

"I will not believe it until I see the proof." His word was final.

# Chapter Six

"Bloody magistrate," Jane cursed under her breath. She modified her tone, wanting him to listen. "I will do what I can to find out what Lydia's up to that's endangering her. But my advice was sincere; Ramsay, you really need to pay her more attention."

"Stop calling me Ramsay," he grumbled. He further untidied his auburn hair, giving it the appearance of a mop, and took a deep breath. "Forgive me, I am being beastly. You are a trial to me, Miss Leighton, but I do appreciate your offer of help."

Jane managed to smile. "See? That's exactly the kind of behavior Lydia needs to see."

He gave her an unfathomable look and rose, moving away from her. "It is late. I'm sure you wish a few hours of sleep before sunrise?"

He made sure she safely reached his bedroom before crossing the hallway to his temporary sleeping quarters.

"Good night, Mr. Chadwick," she called softly after him.

He twisted, his shoulders hunching almost defensively. "Ah—ah, good night, Miss Leighton."

* * *

Ramsay's clerk appeared in his dining room the following morning waving a handful of bank notes.

Ramsay lowered his knife and fork to his plate, placing the silver-toned cutlery at a precise angle to each other. "A gambling win?" he joked lightly.

Mr. Allsop glared at him, the severity softened by their difference in status. "These were handed to me this morning, sir. They're fake."

"Forgeries?" Ramsay examined them. "They're good but not good enough. Where did you get them?"

"Jamison the tailor. Yesterday he tried to collect on the outstanding bills for the last quarter. Those bank notes could've come from any number of places."

He heard his assistant's unspoken criticism: all possible sources belonged to the elite of Bath society. Ramsay handed them back. "You know what you have to do. Get a list of those who paid yesterday and investigate. See where else this money is turning up. We'll find them."

Jane changed into one of her new Regency-style gowns. Pulling on her gloves, she heard someone knock softly on her door.

"Only me, dear," Mrs. Marshall said when Jane opened her door. "You have a phone call." She smiled. "Going out again? You look lovely, dear."

Descending to the ground floor, Jane picked up the receiver. It felt odd to talk on the phone while dressed in gear designed for a century before its invention. "Hello?"

"Jane? It's Patricia. What are you doing in Bath?"

"Relaxing." Jane thought the question rather odd. Patricia knew why.

"And the rest." Patricia snorted. "I had another dream about you last night."

"Patricia . . ." Jane warned.

"And what with Terrance showing up at work the other day, I thought I'd do your chart."

Jane sighed in defeat. "And what do the stars say?"

"That's just it, Jane. I've never seen an astrology chart less clear before. Everything's all mixed up. I took it to Bridget—" Bridget was her mentor in the New Age arts. "She's just as confused. It's like you're not there half the time, and the rest is a frenzy of activity."

"Well, I have been doing some research about a past resident of this place. You know me—I have to keep busy," Jane admitted, leaning against the wall. How strange, she thought, that Patricia's star chart saw she traveled through time.

"Yet most of the stars are in the emotional quadrant of the sky. It's weird, Jane. I checked all my calculations and they're right, but they don't make sense. There's one thing that is clear, and that's why I called to tell you . . ." Her friend's voice trailed away.

"Tell me what?"

"That if you don't sort out this emotional mess—and I'm guessing this means Terrance, although the stars are suggesting someone new . . . That if you don't sort it out, someone's going to die."

Jane's legs went wobbly and she clutched the telephone tighter. "What?"

"That's what's really messed up. Someone's going to die or is dead already. It's so weird. Jane, be careful."

Jane bit her lip. Patricia wouldn't have called unless it was serious, unless it was very personal, which discounted the already dead Ramsay, whose death she wanted to delay. "Is it— is it me?"

Silence came from Patricia's end. "Even if I could answer a question like that," she replied, her voice low, "I can't. It's just not clear. Be careful, Jane—or better yet—come home."

"I'll be fine," Jane reassured her, feeling anything but. She rang off and returned upstairs to wait for the sunset, determined to dismiss Patricia's woo-woo worries.

She'd never thought to check: did time move the same for him as it did to her? Could his days be racing past in the space of her single day? How long did she really have?

Clutching the bedpost, Jane sagged with relief on seeing Ramsay appear, pacing the carpet before her.

"Please hurry," he said, pulling her to her feet. "Lydia and her mother arrived half an hour ago. If I delay any longer, they shall come to see what delays us."

His brusque, careless attitude was just what she needed to brush away the last of Patricia's bugaboos. "Have I had a headache today?"

"Yes, but you feel well enough for dinner. I have come up to discover the reason for your tardiness."

"That was kind of you." Jane looped her arm through his. "Shall we go down?"

He glanced at her as they descended the stairs. "You seem particularly calm today, Miss Leighton."

"I've been practicing being suitable for the upper echelons of Bath society." She flashed him a strained smile. "Being able to come back here tonight is an utter relief."

"Did you discover any new information about . . ." he trailed off.

"Nothing conclusive," she hedged. She had to speak to Lydia first, privately if possible. "Could you entertain Mrs. Devereaux tonight? I need to talk with your fiancée privately."

His brow furrowed. "Lydia may not wish to—"

"She will." Jane grinned. "You underestimate my powers."

His frown deepened. "That's what I am afraid of."

He led her into the drawing room. She recognized it at once as Ramsay's makeshift ballroom, now restored to its original use. A small piano stood in one corner near the large windows, and a sofa and Hepplewhite chairs lined the walls. Without the press of people, she saw the room's main feature, a fireplace of white and variegated marble.

She exchanged pleasantries with the Devereauxs and dodged an inquiry after her chaperone.

"She is still feeling poorly," Jane supplied, sitting in a chair next to the sofa. She hoped she covered Ramsay's startled expression. It was clear he hadn't thought of a chaperone.

True to his word, he endeavored to draw Mrs. Devereaux away from her and Lydia. Jane flashed him a thankful smile, as she had been caught up in an inconsequential conversation about the sights of Bath.

"What did you say to him?" Lydia's abrupt change of the topic indicated she too had been waiting for a quiet moment.

"Say to who? Ramsay?"

"Mr. Chadwick." Lydia's eyes narrowed.

*Oops.* Jane smiled. She needed to head off any suspicions on Lydia's part because of her gaffe. "I only mentioned he should pay more attention to you. I wanted to help. Why? What has he done?"

"He is paying more attention to me," Lydia complained.

So he had taken her advice after all! Triumphant, she buried a laugh. "And you don't like that?" She sipped at her tea.

"It is not that . . ." Lydia trailed off and leaned forward. "You will not tell him this, will you? I can trust you with my secret?"

"I won't tell him," Jane vowed, hanging on Lydia's every word. "I swear it."

Lydia settled back, apparently mollified by her answer. "I am not marrying him out of love, you understand. It is to please my parents."

"You are a very dutiful daughter," Jane remarked cautiously. "I think I would rather be unmarried than live with a man I couldn't love."

Lydia gazed across the room where Ramsay labored through

a discussion with her mother. "Please understand, I do not dislike him. He is pleasant to look at." She sighed and faced Jane. "But he is not very exciting."

*Pleasant?* The thought blazed across Jane's mind. *He's a darn sight more than pleasant to look at!* She tried not to let her amazement show. She chewed the inside of her lip. "I've heard it said that those in arranged marriages do end up finding, if not love, then deep affection for each other." She lowered her voice, leaning closer. "He loves you, you know. The battle is half-won there. Whatever you do, don't make him hate you."

Lydia's lack of reaction to her warning worried Jane.

Mrs. Devereaux rejoined them, Ramsay trailing behind. "Lydia, my dear, why don't you play the pianoforte for Mr. Chadwick's charming cousin?"

Lydia made a face. "Perhaps Miss Leighton would prefer to play, Mama."

"Oh no," Jane hastily interjected before Mrs. Devereaux could remonstrate with her daughter. "I can't play a note!"

Mrs. Devereaux nodded. "Do not be so modest, Miss Leighton. We will hear you play in due course. Lydia, if you please."

Without further protest, Lydia did her mother's bidding, settling herself at the piano. She started by playing a soft sonata.

Jane caught her breath. The music was exquisite, although it sounded more like a harpsichord than a piano. She glanced at Ramsay. He seemed entranced by Lydia's music-making. A swift look at Mrs. Devereaux showed her well pleased with Ramsay's rapt expression.

She stirred not an iota from where she sat, not wanting to distract Ramsay from Lydia. For once, the two seemed to be in complete harmony.

Her nose itched, threatening a sneeze. She looked down at the gorgeous red and pale green rug carpeting the floorboards, holding her breath. If she moved, would he look at her and break the spell? She choked back a snort. Ramsay was not interested in her, nor did she want him to be. Why would he even care if she scratched her nose?

She lifted her hand to rub at the offending member, turning her head away from the assembled group.

Her eyes widened. Mark Darby leaned against the door lintel, listening to Lydia play with an expression identical to Ramsay's.

She lowered her gaze, stunned by the naked longing in Darby's face. Ramsay's best friend loved Lydia. No wonder he sought her out. Was it a harmless attraction, one kept in check out of respect for Ramsay? Or did he plan on stealing her right from under Ramsay's nose?

That all depended, she imagined, on how Lydia felt about Mr. Darby. She turned back to the piano. Lydia, focused on her playing, hadn't yet seen the new arrival. From all appearances, music seemed one of her great loves. No wonder Ramsay owned a piano for her to perform upon.

Lydia finished the piece and surveyed her audience. She saw the new arrival. A smile broke out, hastily reined in. "Mr. Darby!"

"Miss Devereaux." Mark Darby bowed from where he stood. "I didn't wish to interrupt you."

Lydia gracefully rose from the piano stool and crossed to him. "How sweet of you to come!" Her arm in his, she drew him into the room. Her vibrancy, tonight seen only while she played, returned in full force. "Mr. Chadwick, you didn't tell me Mr. Darby would be joining us this evening."

Ramsay frowned. "That's because I did not know it." His smile thinned, all traces of pleasure gone. "Mr. Darby, are you planning on staying? Shall I order another place setting for you?"

Darby grinned. "I'm famished."

Ramsay crossed to the fireplace and rang the silken bell pull dangling there.

Jane remained motionless, awash in disappointment. All her guidance would be useless if Lydia had set her heart on another.

Mrs. Devereaux coughed, her brows lowered. Lydia abandoned Mark Darby and crossed to Ramsay, who relaxed once her hand rested on his arm.

A male servant appeared in the doorway. "Yes, sir?" he asked with a slight bow.

"Have another place set for Mr. Darby," Ramsay instructed.

"Dinner is ready, Mr. Chadwick. If you wait but another moment, I'll have Mr. Darby's place ready."

Jane felt the servant's curious gaze upon her. And why shouldn't he be curious? For someone who purportedly lived in the house, she was never seen except in the evening.

Mr. Darby led Mrs. Devereaux into dinner, leaving Jane to trail behind alone and in last place. She didn't mind.

Dinner was a quiet affair, the conversation stilted. A heavy pall of disapproval hung over the table, most of it from Mrs. Devereaux. Not even Lydia and Mark remained oblivious to the tension.

Jane saw how Mark gazed at Lydia with a hungry expression. Aside from a few glances, Lydia ignored him, but she answered all questions in monosyllables.

She stared at the sand-colored walls, not feeling exactly talkative either. Not that anyone seemed interested in talking with her.

As the meal drew to an end, Lydia pleaded a headache. She turned soulful, apologetic eyes upon Ramsay. "I am so sorry," she said, "but perhaps Miss Leighton's headache is catching."

"I hope not," Jane blurted, watching a spasm of distaste cross Ramsay's face. He knew the headache excuse for a lie.

Mark Darby rose. "Mrs. Devereaux, allow me to escort you and your daughter home." Mrs. Devereaux demurred, but

Darby persisted. "We will be traveling the same way. I assure you it will not be an imposition."

"Mama," Lydia murmured, laying a hand on her mother's arm. "Please do not argue; it makes my headache worse."

Jane remained at the table, Ramsay leaving to bid them farewell. She propped her head on her hands, her elbows on the table, gloomily observing her reflection in the highly polished mahogany. Lydia could turn an entire room to her whim. Why didn't she have that knack? Worse, the girl had engineered more time with Darby.

She looked up when Ramsay returned. "I am glad Mrs. Devereaux did not see you like that," he said. "You would have been undone."

Jane straightened, grimacing at his stern features.

He resumed his seat, his cold expression dropping away to reveal his desolation. "This is bad, isn't it."

If any man needed a hug . . . She brushed the thought away. "Could be." Jane bit her lower lip, thinking how best to approach it. "I don't suppose there's the slightest chance Lydia and Darby were childhood chums or are related?"

"No." Ramsay's voice hardened, his complexion reddening with repressed anger. "What did you see?"

"Two people in love with each other yet not ready to admit it," Jane replied frankly. "And I don't mean you and Lydia."

A soft groan escaped his lips, which he clamped shut. "Darby denies it. I asked him."

"So you *have* sensed it." Her heart plummeted. If Ramsay had guessed it, she hadn't been mistaken. "And of course he would deny it. He's your friend; he doesn't want to hurt you."

Ramsay rose and stalked from the table, examining a still life painting of a vase of roses. His stiff bearing resonated with hurt.

Jane joined him, lightly touching his shoulders, uncertain of how to offer her sympathy. He shrugged them off. She murmured, needing to give him hope, "They haven't admitted it yet, Ramsay. That's out of respect for you."

"What do I do?" he ground out between his teeth.

"Woo her again. Sweetly and gently. Never leave her side. Do not gift her with expensive trinkets but with wildflowers and ribbons."

"I would give her the world, Miss Leighton."

She took a deep breath, shaken by the depth of his declaration. "Then let her in, Ramsay. Let her see you vulnerable; let her help you solve a problem. Perhaps there's a recent case involving a woman, and you need her particular female wisdom?"

He turned his head in her direction. "You think this will keep her alive?"

"And you," she reminded him. "What would you have done otherwise? Kept going on as you are, distant and authoritative?" He winced at her sharp words. "She wants someone to fall in love with, to romance her."

"Like those silly gothic novels she reads?"

"Those novels are not all silly. Have you read *Pride and Prejudice?*"

Huffing with impatience, Ramsay shook his head.

"Is it out?"

"By that, do you mean has it been published? I do not know. I can ask at the bookseller's." His stiff demeanor hadn't slackened.

"Ramsay . . ."

"Will you stop calling me that!" he snapped. "Remember your position."

Her jaw dropped, staring at him. She just wanted to help, to make him feel better. *Idiot,* she told herself. "Fine. Be like that. If you do not need my help anymore, I'll go upstairs and wait for the dawn." She turned and strode from the room.

She reached the door and glanced back. Ramsay hadn't

moved, standing with his hand concealing his eyes, his shoulders hunched and tense.

*Jane, you are a sucker for a sad guy.* Sighing, she returned to him, standing close but not daring to touch him. "Mr. Chadwick. Forgive me; my time is really informal when it comes to names."

He didn't respond.

"Perhaps we could talk about your recent cases as magistrate? I thought maybe one of the cases might have a bearing on your and Lydia's disappearances."

"How could that be?" He relented, curiosity getting the better of him.

She winced. "Because I just suggested that you talk to her about them. Time travel is an awful paradox. I may be saving you or . . . or not."

His eyes grew wide. "You never mentioned this before."

"It never occurred to me before." She hung her head. "Perhaps this isn't a good idea after all."

He shook his head. "I don't believe that. You were the only ghost who has come to life. There has to be a reason for that."

Lines drew down the sides of his mouth. He looked years older. She knew he didn't want to be alone. She was his only ally. "You think so?"

"I have to hope so." He swallowed. "I know how to pay attention to a woman, to flatter her, but Lydia receives such attentions all the time."

"Then praise not her eyes or her hair but her mind."

"Her mind?" He looked at her, startled. "I'm not marrying her for that!"

She restrained the urge to hit him, but only just. "Mr. Chadwick," she began, aware she sounded like her mother. "If you are to woo a woman successfully, you must want her: body, mind and soul. Not just the pretty one-third."

His brow creased in puzzlement. "How do I praise her mind?"

Jane sighed. This would take forever. "Well, what do you talk about with her?"

He had to think. "The wedding plans, the country house I have bought for her, how she would decorate it."

"Then praise her management skills. Putting a wedding together is no small feat. Praise her style in decorating. Take her shopping for household items. Praise her financial sense, if she has one."

His brows lowered. "You sound doubtful on that score."

She refused to be cowed. "She's young. She may not have developed one. The young don't think of their future."

"You are not that old."

She managed a smile. "Thank you. If her mother's careful, chances are she will be too."

"Anything else?" A jaw-splitting yawn punctuated his question. "My pardon, that was ill-mannered of me."

"Have you slept at all?" she queried, frowning.

"A little, not much," he admitted, brushing away her concern with a wave of his hand. "There is a case demanding much of my attention and I cannot afford to let it slip."

"You should rest. A yawning suitor is scarcely flattering." She laid a hand on his arm, withdrawing it at his sharp look. "What is this case about?"

He arched a brow. "I scarcely see how that matters."

"It might have a connection to your disappearance. If I could find out the results . . ."

"Miss Leighton, I see and judge up to twenty cases a day. Some cases are examined over a number of days. I cannot give you my register—"

"I thought magistrates didn't start keeping registers until the 1870s?"

His eyes widened at that. "I follow the example of the Fieldings. They were meticulous in everything they did."

Jane would not be distracted by a historical footnote, no matter how fascinating. "Copy down the major cases then. I know a historian. He should be able to help me find out what happened." She paused. "Of course, I cannot influence history and tell you of your future decisions, but if it is a lead, it could be vital. It could provide a hint, especially depending on what happened after."

"Miss Leighton, you are rambling." Did she detect a hint of amusement in his voice? "Perhaps we should retire for the night."

The image of her retiring *with* Ramsay flashed across her mind, and just as quickly, she banished it. She followed him upstairs, trying to ignore the flexing of his supple calf beneath the tight white stockings. Even in old-fashioned breeches, he looked yummy.

It was a good thing, she reflected, that they belonged to two different eras. She had to remember her goal was his happiness, not a temporary lift in hers.

Murmuring good night, Ramsay crossed the hallway to the guest bedroom. Jane pushed on the doorknob to her room. "Miss Leighton?" He retraced his steps, a charged light in his eye, although confusion lined his brow.

"Yes, Mr. Chadwick?" Despite her cool words, something in his eyes made her heart thud.

"Your words of advice . . ." He paused, the slightest hint of a head shake indicating he didn't wish to proceed with this line of conversation, even though he had started it. His chest puffed with a steadying breath. "I take it they come from experience?"

"Experience?" Jane knew from her Heyer and Austen how the Regency era treated 'experienced' girls, but she decided to be frank. Better for him to have the truth, and why not—there were no expectations between them. Yet she had to put it into his era's terms. Speaking *too* frankly would shock him. "I have been unlucky in love, Mr. Chadwick. I have been successfully wooed and seduced by unscrupulous characters who were found out to be married, or unfaithful, or just very, very strange." She shivered, remembering Terrance who fit all three criteria.

"Do not your parents approve your suitors?" he asked, puzzled.

She laughed at the thought of it. Oh, her mother would like to see her fixed up and birthing grandkids, but she had never *really* interfered. "It is not done that way in my time. We women fend for ourselves."

His frown grew deeper. "That doesn't seem right. A defenseless woman on her own? Doesn't your own experience show how inadvisable that is?"

"I've been unlucky," she reiterated. "I seem to attract the wrong kind of man, the unavailable kind. Yes, I get hurt, but I recover." She wondered if she had convinced him. Her lips tightened, the wounds still too raw for her to believe that she could recover.

He gave an abrupt nod. "I see. I shall bid you a good night again, Miss Leighton."

She watched him go, wondering if he now hated her for her "fallen" state.

Ramsay, sitting on the edge of his narrow bed in the prettily wallpapered but rarely used guest bedroom, rubbed his chin. The future that Jane—Miss Leighton—came from was very strange indeed.

A woman of her history would not be tolerated at all by him or his class, and yet, despite her madcap tendencies, she had a strong moral sense. She'd vowed to help him gain a successful marriage to Lydia, putting aside all her own concerns.

He knew they existed from the odd way she spoke of her past. He knew little of such couplings, but he'd wager she was escaping a recent encounter. It didn't please him that one of his theories about her as a ghost had a ring of truth.

Was she using his troubles to redeem herself?

His smile twisted. He didn't mind if that were true. He needed all the help he could get.

Trenby, his valet, entered and Ramsay allowed himself to be undressed and prepared for bed. "Sir . . ." Trenby began.

"Yes?" Ramsay shrugged himself into his nightshirt.

"Regarding Miss Leighton . . ."

"I thought I left instructions that Miss Leighton's presence was not to be questioned," he snapped.

"She is not in your—her room during the day. Where does she go?"

"What did I say about questions?" He grimaced and relented. Trenby was a good and faithful man. He deserved a little more, and he could rely on Trenby's discretion. "You need not have any concerns about Miss Leighton. She may be unusual, but her character is impeccable—"

"How can that be? She is here without a chaperone!"

"Not as far as the world knows—and I want it kept that way. You know I have not taken her as a lover." The thought gave his blood an unexpected surge. He damped down the notion. Impossible. It would take more than a pretty leg to turn him from his Lydia!

He continued. "My relationship with Miss Leighton is completely platonic. She is here to help, not to complicate matters, understand? I'd appreciate it if you quashed any of the servants' gossip. Make sure no one goes into that room, is that clear? Not even to clean the fireplace."

"I will lock it, sir, and inform the others your cousin is not to be disturbed." Trenby paused, digesting his litany of requests. "She's not your cousin though, is she?"

Trenby had reached the heart of the matter as usual. Ramsay schooled his features into a soothing blank. "No, she is not."

Jane didn't mean to yawn just as Mrs. Marshall came out with breakfast but it was too late to hide it.

"The ghost still?" Mrs. Marshall asked with a deep frown of concern.

"Not so much," Jane hedged. "I don't mind him, truly."

Mrs. Marshall remained unconvinced. "Perhaps I should have Father Doherty come in and—"

"No!" Jane exclaimed, horrified at the thought of Ramsay being wiped out of existence. "You can't do that!"

"But you're not sleeping, dear."

"I have other . . . problems. It's not entirely due to his ghost. In fact, he helps me forget about them. Please don't call in a priest." Jane considered getting on her knees and begging the woman. She couldn't lose Ramsay now. He needed her!

Mrs. Marshall promised.

He needed her in a most platonic way, Jane reminded herself. "Besides," she added, "think of the benefit the B&B would have. A ghost would be a selling point."

"Hmm," Mrs. Marshall mused, "perhaps I should see if I can be included on the Haunted Walking Tour." She wandered off to the kitchen deep in thought.

Jane finished breakfast and headed out, making a beeline for Bath's downtown shopping district. If she was going to help Ramsay, then she needed to seek advice. What better place than the bookshop's self help section?

Maybe she could find something for herself while she was there. *28 Easy Ways to Spot a Married Man,* perhaps, or *How to Find a Man Who'll Commit,* as opposed to one who needed to be committed.

With a rueful smile, she entered W.H. Smith's, strolling along the aisles until she found what she wanted.

She skipped past all the *Chicken Soup . . . for various souls.* Warm colors of reds and yellows leapt out at her. These were the colors of love and romance. Why did all the love and romance advice books have such corny titles and covers?

She moved to the next shelf and scanned the titles. Looking closer, almost all of the books were directed at women, dedicated to helping them get their man. *But how,* Jane wondered, thumbing through one of the books, *does a man get his woman? Does it just work out if she's more desperate?*

She reached for a book on the top shelf. A familiar uncombed crown of dark brown hair appeared on the other side.

Jane hunched her shoulders. Surely, there were plenty of guys with dark brown hair and a huge cowlick on his pate? She shivered. It *was* him. She knew it. How many times had she combed her fingers through that hair?

The wedding ring on his finger hadn't stopped him from pursuing her, and he had followed her here . . .

At a crouch, she scurried along the aisle and dashed out of the store.

Peeking over her shoulder, she saw Terrance look her way. He took one step, then two toward her.

He saw her. He knew her. He was coming after her.

Jane fled through the mall, her heart pounding. She ducked down a narrow lane, across a busy street, and into another lane, her plimsolls slapping against the cobblestones. At the next street, she turned right, away from the bed and breakfast, and ducked into a shop.

She hurried to the back of the shop, prepared to duck behind a clothing rack, and surveyed the street.

She didn't see him. She hovered, nervously fingering the fine silk garment before her without even looking at it. He couldn't be far behind if he had given chase.

"May I help you?" A shop assistant approached.

Jane flashed her a frightened look. "A man is following me. Do you mind if I hide out here for a while?"

The shop assistant laughed throatily. "Of course not. There's no chance he'd come in here looking for you."

For the first time, Jane took in her environs. Her refuge sold lingerie. She snatched up the pale blue creation she'd been fingering. "Thanks. I'll go try this on."

The shop assistant looked her over and tut-tutted. "Not your size. Try this."

Didn't the woman understand she wanted to hide? Jane grabbed the proffered undergarment and headed into the changing room. Terrance wouldn't find her here.

She sat, the lingerie item discarded beside her, for half an hour. Leaning back against the wall, she closed her eyes and tried to think about Ramsay's problems, not her own. What else could she suggest to bring him and Lydia closer together?

A brief thought flashed through her mind. What would Ramsay say if he saw her in the silky teddy she hadn't even tried on? He'd be lost for words. He didn't seem the sort to have seen a woman in something that skimpy.

But he never would because like all men, he wasn't for her.

# Chapter Seven

Jane greeted sunset with enthusiasm. She'd made her escape from the lingerie shop and returned to the bed and breakfast confident she hadn't been followed. Terrance might know she was in Bath, but he didn't yet know where she stayed.

Ramsay entered the bedchamber. She swung her feet off the bed, ready to join him. Their hands joined in practiced unison, and she rose off the bed and into 1812.

"What are our plans tonight?" She blinked, adjusting her eyes to the candlelight.

He stepped back, giving her some room. He didn't appear to be in any hurry. "Miss Lydia appears to be otherwise engaged this evening."

Jane raised an eyebrow. "Doing what?"

He gave an elegant shrug, turning to brush invisible dust off the mantel. "I cannot say. She accepted my invitation to dinner tomorrow night. I need your suggestions. What can I do to make it a romantic evening?"

"Don't invite Darby."

Ramsay winced.

She shot him an apologetic look, thinking over this fresh problem. She'd seen something in those books at the store.

What was it? She grinned. "I have it. Do you have something called fondue?"

He frowned. "Perhaps. Describe it."

"It's a cheese and wine sauce. You dip bread squares and suchlike into it."

"Sounds like the old peasant dish." His lip curled.

"Probably." Jane didn't see the reason for his distaste. "But it's very tasty. You could feed the bread to her."

This alone seemed to interest Ramsay. He thumbed his lower lip, moving closer. "Your experience is proving useful. But her mother—"

Jane gave it to him straight. "I suggest you talk to Mrs. Devereaux about your concerns regarding Lydia's wandering affections."

"That sounds dreadfully gauche." He looked half-hopeful.

"So? I'd bet you a penny for a pound that Mrs. Devereaux will leap at the chance for you and her daughter to spend some time alone. You have a larger fortune than Darby, correct?"

He nodded, the hope fading from his face. "You're suggesting that the match was made for monetary reasons."

She laid her hand on his arm. "Ramsay, you really must read Austen. 'It is a truth universally acknowledged, that a single man in possession of a good fortune, must be in want of a wife.'"

He drew back, affronted. "Lydia is not after my money."

Jane didn't have the heart to break it to him. Besides, she needed to get the two of them together, not plant seeds of doubt. She gazed at the brocade of his waistcoat. "Every young prospective bride gets hit by unreasonable fears, no matter how much in love she is with the groom. This is when she needs the evidence of your love for her, to make her feel secure that she's made the right choice."

His shoulders remained at stiff angles. Didn't he ever relax? "And her flirtation with Darby?"

"Could be nothing more than wanting to make you jealous and to be sure of your love." She hoped that sounded confident.

He unbent a little. "You really think so?"

Jane sighed. "I don't know Lydia very well yet, but from what I've seen, she loves to flirt. She knows she has power over men. Flirting is harmless so long as she's with you." She looked up, intent on making her point, and realized too late that they had moved quite close together. Too close.

She swallowed and side-stepped around him. "Why don't we give the fondue a trial run?" she said lightly. "See if you think it is right for you and Lydia."

"You want us to have a romantic meal?" He tracked her progress away from him. Her cheeks flushed at his wide-eyed incredulous attention.

"Of course not," Jane replied, indignant. "I can show you a few tricks, and you can practice feeding another woman. I assume you've not done something like this before?"

Ramsay demurred. "There seemed no reason to."

She headed for the door. "Then let's see if your cook knows how to make it."

He followed her downstairs. "Jane—Miss Leighton—one does not go into the kitchen to speak with the cook. One summons her."

She delivered a look over her shoulder, considered saying something sharp, but thought better of it. "Whatever you say, Mr. Chadwick."

His cook, a thin woman, joined them in his study. Ramsay opened the interview. "Miss Leighton wishes to be served fondue this evening. Do you know how to make that?"

"Make it?" The cook clasped her hands in front of her. "Of course I do! And a delicious soufflé it is too."

Jane corrected her. "The dish I mean is a cheese and wine sauce used for dipping."

The cook's white cap concealed even the slightest wisp of

hair. She stared. "But, beggin' yer pardon, that's a common dish! Mr. Chadwick, I know ye've been generous and kind to Miss Leighton, but—"

"That will do." Ramsay's mouth hardened, quashing any remaining protest. "If you can make it, please do so. Miss Leighton assures me it will be a delightful meal to share with Miss Devereaux tête-à-tête, and I apparently need to practice."

The cook gave Jane a long, measuring stare. "So that's the way of it, is it?" The cook smiled, clearly forgiving her for her uncouth request, as they shared a common goal in making her master happy. "Then it shall be so!"

Curtseying, she bustled out of the room.

Jane turned to Ramsay. "Now we need to lay a tablecloth on the dining room floor." She left his study and headed for the dining room.

"On the floor?" He trailed after her.

"I said this was an intimate meal, didn't I?" she shot over her shoulder. She halted just inside the dining room, surveying the room. At the same time, she was aware of Ramsay stopping short very close behind her. "We shall have to move the dining table and perhaps remove some of the table leaves."

Saying this, she ducked under the table, searching for the lever.

"Miss Leighton, what are you doing?"

She glanced at his shiny boots. "There should be something that unlocks the leaves . . ."

"Miss Leighton, please get out from under the table. I'll ring for some footmen to prepare the room."

She wondered how it was possible that shoes could look so annoyed. She crawled out from under the table and rose, automatically dusting off her hands. "Don't you do anything yourself?"

"I try cases. That is my area of expertise." He tugged on a

bell-pull by the fireplace. "I leave other things to those who know what they're doing."

At length, the dining room was prepared for their feast. A white linen tablecloth lay spread on the floorboards, a rug adding a cushion. A candelabra, wine glasses, and two small plates rested on the tablecloth. Long forks had been found for dipping.

The sauce itself was brought in by the cook, who entered the dining room laden with a chafing dish. Bread cubes were delivered in a bowl by one of the maids.

"Is this all?" Ramsay asked, staring at the simple fare before them.

"Oh, I'm sure you and your cook can figure out something more to add to the dish." Jane sat on the floor, curling her heels beneath her. "Asparagus would work too, or broccoli. Various cooked vegetables." She winked at the departing cook, amused to see the wink returned. "But we'll practice on bread for now."

Jane speared a bread cube. That was the easy part. Dipping it into the cheese sauce and transferring it to her mouth were the tricky parts. A light dipping and curling her wrist captured any drippings before they landed on either the tablecloth or her.

She chewed and swallowed. "Mmm, this is good." She held out the other fork. "Come on, try it."

Ramsay awkwardly crouched down, landing on one knee before settling onto the tablecloth. "This is most irregular," he muttered.

"Yes," she agreed, watching his limbs rearrange themselves into careless elegance. "And that's what will make it so attractive to Lydia." She watched as he speared a bread cube and dipped it into the fondue. "Try a little more sauce next time."

He did as he was bid, licking his upper lip to retrieve a smear of cheesy sauce. He looked to her for approval.

Jane licked her own lips. Her breath caught a little. Here

she was, sitting on the floor with a handsome man, teaching him how to woo another.

*The things we do to salve our conscience,* she thought. "Now," she said aloud, fixing a bright smile on her face. She wouldn't let him see she'd been caught up by him. "Let's see how you do feeding Lydia."

Ramsay dunked the bread into the fondue with confidence, twirling the fork to catch the dripping. His fork swooped toward her mouth. She parted her lips eagerly. This was as close to romantic as she would ever get.

The bread made it successfully into her mouth. The cheese however . . . It dribbled down her chin. Pulling back, she caught up the offending cheese and scooped it into her mouth.

"Close," she said, grinning at his consternation. "Try again."

With his breaded fork, he gave the sauce pot a few stirs, before twirling the fork free. "Lean forward," he commanded.

She obeyed, ready to catch the morsel. He moved too fast, causing the cheese sauce to spatter across her cream satin bodice. "Oh dear!" She laughed, grabbing a napkin and patting at the hot cheese. "Any higher and you could have licked it off Lydia's bosom."

He flushed scarlet. "Let me try again." His voice trembled. Perhaps she shouldn't have put the idea of licking bosoms into his mind.

His third attempt was no better. His hand shook a little. The cheese spattered across her skirt.

Dabbing at her skirt, she reached forward and grasped his wrist, preventing him from feeding her again. "I think it's time for my revenge. If you would allow me to demonstrate."

She slowed her movements and became (she hoped) graceful. With a ginger dip of the bread chunk into the sauce, she lifted it free of the fondue and paused, letting it drip. She glanced over at Ramsay and found him mesmerized by her actions.

The tempo of her heart increased. Was it she he had become absorbed by, or was it merely her technique? In her haste to shake the thought from her mind, she almost shoved the bread in the direction of his mouth, and the cheese spattered across his coat.

He chewed and swallowed the bread, his eyes narrowing. "You meant to do that," he accused.

"No!" she protested, in danger of laughing, her eyes wide. "I swear!"

"A likely tale, Miss Leighton." Deadpan, he dipped his fork, sans bread, into the cheese sauce and flicked it at her.

She squealed with shocked laughter. "Right. This means war."

Her fork plunged into the fondue, and he vaulted over the pot, showing none of his earlier awkwardness. She managed to fling a forkful at him before he wrestled her arm back over her head.

He straddled her, holding her arms down. She struggled against him, her laughter mixing in with his soft chuckles. "You are a minx, Jane." He recaptured a wrist that threatened to escape him.

He leaned over her. The pounding of her heart, at first sparked by the adrenaline rush of an innocent wrestle, thumped harder with a deeper emotion.

"You're not playing fair," she accused, trying to keep things light and easy. They didn't need to get complicated. Not now. "I got more cheese on me than you did."

"Yes, but it was an accident when I did it."

Gazing up at him, she saw the exact moment when Ramsay started thinking again. His fair-skinned face darkened. "Surrender, Miss Leighton," he growled.

"And what happens when I surrender?" she challenged him, breathless with the possibilities.

Wrong question.

He let her go. Catapulting to his feet, he distanced himself from her and the ruins of their meal.

Jane struggled into a sitting position, watching his retreat. "We must be careful, Mr. Chadwick," she murmured, watching the torment play across his features. "Sometimes the play-acting seems real."

She rose, ignoring the cheesy stains on her gown. She'd take it to the dry cleaners tomorrow. She focused on Ramsay who'd turned his back to her.

"It's not real," she murmured, wanting to soothe him. "It cannot be real. It is Lydia you love. I've seen it with my own eyes."

"And—and that?" He pointed vaguely behind him at the crumpled tablecloth on the floor.

She thought fast. "An animal instinct perhaps. We both sensed it and fought it off. We both know it to be wrong."

She wished he'd face her so she could read his features. He mustn't doubt his love for Lydia. She couldn't ruin another relationship. For the first time, she had done the right thing and not acted upon her attraction. She couldn't let his doubts ruin him.

"Ramsay—Mr. Chadwick," she pleaded.

He turned and faced her, his features like cold marble. "Miss Leighton, I think it is time you retired for the evening."

She stooped into a brief curtsey. He had it all under control then. "Good evening, Mr. Chadwick." She matched his cool tones.

She retreated to the dining room door, turning back as a thought occurred to her. He stared after her with a naked longing, quickly masked at her turn. She wished she hadn't seen it, thrilled that she had.

"Mr. Chadwick?" She cursed the sound of her breathlessness. She didn't even have the excuse of a corset. "Did you remember to get me that list of cases?"

He nodded stiffly and pulled a folded paper from his coat's

breast pocket. Closing the distance between them, he handed it to her.

The paper was still warm from his body. She unfolded it, her fingers trembling a little, and skimmed the contents. "And I thought nineteenth-century handwriting was impossible to read," she remarked, folding the paper and tucking it into her bodice.

She looked up to see his gaze follow the path his list had taken.

He cleared his throat. "Is that so?"

"Yes." She grinned at him. "It's only almost impossible to read."

She saw a ghost of his smile, and satisfied with that, retreated to her bedroom. At least she would get one night's rest.

In the privacy of his bedchamber, she read the list more closely. How could any of them involve Lydia? The list was rather mundane: burglaries, forged bank notes, and petty thieving. How then had they disappeared?

The following morning, intent on returning to the office of Mr. Jenkins, the historian, Jane walked out of the B&B and right into Terrance.

"There you are." Terrance's smile frightened her with its intensity. "I've been looking for you."

How dare he ruin her holiday! She kept him at arm's length. "Well, now that you've found me, you can go away again. It's over, Terrance. How many times do I have to tell you?"

"It's not over until I say it is." He grabbed her hand. She struggled to free herself from his tight grip. "You're making a scene," he continued coolly. "Why don't I buy you a drink and we can talk about this?"

Jane gave up struggling. For the moment. She'd give him one last chance to let her go, and then there'd be hell to pay.

"There's nothing to talk about. If you don't let me go this instant, I will make a scene. I'm warning you, Terrance, don't make me do this."

"You wouldn't." Without even waiting to see if she would, he hauled her across the broad, flat paving stones toward a car.

Letting out a frightened shriek, she fought him. "Help! Rape!"

Yet it was quiet, too quiet on the Crescent that morning, her yells swallowed up in the great breadth of space. A couple in the distance appeared at the far edge of the green walking a dog.

He dragged her toward the end of the Crescent, away from the city. She looked behind her. Not even a curtain flickered.

His fingers dug deeper into her upper arm and he swung her around, trying to silence her mouth with his hand. She flung all her weight into elbowing him and he let her go with an "oof."

She sprinted back across the Crescent's curve, returning to the sanctuary of the bed and breakfast.

Slamming the door behind her, she leaned against it, panting, hearing the deadlock snap into place.

Her relief evaporated. She wouldn't stay here. Terrance knew where she was now. She could never be safe again. What was she to do?

"Are you all right, dear?" Mrs. Marshall appeared on the stairs.

"Someone—someone attacked me," Jane gasped out between shuddering breaths.

"Attacked you? On the Crescent?" Mrs. Marshall bolted down the stairs. "I'll call the police."

Jane sank onto the stairs, clutching the newel, while Mrs. Marshall telephoned the police. In the hours that followed, she dutifully gave details of the attack and Terrance's name and description.

At Mrs. Marshall's insistence, the reluctant police officer agreed to double the patrols on the Crescent, warning that there was little that could be done without a restraining order in place.

When they left, Jane called a taxi. Ramsay was relying on her. She needed to see Mr. Jenkins and solve this mystery. Only then could she leave Ramsay to his fate.

"Are you sure you want to go out?" Mrs. Marshall hovered with a cup of tea in her hands, clearly meant for Jane.

Four cups of tea were enough. "There are things I need to do. I'm not going to hide away and ruin the rest of my holiday." She rubbed at her sore arms.

"You're staying?" Mrs. Marshall covered her surprised blurt. "I thought . . . that perhaps you might want to leave . . ."

"Of course I am staying."

Mrs. Marshall bit her lip. "I just called the poltergeist investigators. They were going to investigate Mr. Chadwick's ghost once you'd checked out."

Jane clutched the banister. Would they banish her from her room? From the only reason she stayed on? She tried to hide her consternation. "If you want me to leave, I'll go."

"No, no, don't be silly, dear. Would you mind if they left some equipment in your room?"

Jane shrugged. What would they find? Ramsay wasn't really a ghost. "Not at all. So long as I don't trip over it!"

The two women smiled at each other, a dangerous upset smoothly avoided. In a further concession, Jane sipped at the proffered tea until the taxi arrived.

When she reached Mr. Jenkins's office, nobody answered her knock. The door was unlocked, so she let herself in. Johnny, the historian's assistant, was nowhere in sight.

The historian looked up from rummaging through a crate at the back of the office. "Didn't hear you knock." He grimaced. "Oh, it's you."

She'd rewritten Ramsay's list in her own hand and ballpoint ink. She didn't want to explain his ancient script. She handed it to him. "I found these cases of Rams—Mr. Chadwick's. Could you tell me anything about them?"

He read over the list and then looked down at her over his glasses. "Where did you get this?"

She faked a sigh. "I didn't remember to write down the source. Sorry."

He shook his head at her poor scholarship and handed the list back. "The best you can do is look through the *Bath Journal* or the *Chronicle* in the relevant year and date. You'll find them over at the Bath Central Library." He returned to his crate.

Jane stared at him, open-mouthed. "That's it?" She needed more help than that.

"Afraid so. You'll be doing what I'd pay Johnny to do if you *paid* me to do your research."

She chose to ignore the heavy hint. She didn't have time to wait for Johnny to get back either. "Thanks."

She took her chances and walked through the city to the library. The library formed part of the first floor of "The Podium," a shopping center near the Pulteney Bridge.

The girl at the reference desk directed her to the beige filing cabinets. Soon Jane was hunched over a microfilm machine, ignoring the afternoon sunshine streaming in through the nearby windows.

She turned up a few advertisements asking that the burgled items be returned for rewards. How strange, she thought, that they expected the stolen goods to be returned for a fee. She wondered if the thieves had stolen them only to hold the items for ransom. None of the advertisements mentioned the Devereauxs.

She found even less about the forged bank notes. One notice in the *Advertiser* appealed to all merchants to be wary of the fake bank notes, but nothing else. No arrests, no convictions, nothing.

She approached the librarian and asked for help. "Do you have any records from the Bath magistrates?"

"Magistrates didn't usually keep records," the librarian told her, typing at her terminal. "So I doubt—no, here's something." She wrote the details on a piece of paper. "You should find what you're looking for on these rolls."

Jane retrieved the microfilm and sat down at one of the few readers available. The documents had been scanned in as landscape, so she had to twirl the reel holder by ninety degrees to see the page without cricking her neck.

She squinted at the thick black writing on the projection screen. Whoever had written these had worse handwriting than Ramsay.

The dates at least were legible. She zoomed the machine along until she reached August, 1812. Except for the handwriting, the list matched hers exactly.

Perhaps it wasn't a case that had opened yet, but one closer to the date of his disappearance.

She didn't want to think that he and Lydia had been victims of random violence. How could she prevent that? But that at least left a trace, right. Right?

Maybe they ran off to Jamaica together, she thought with a rueful sigh, and that's why they had left no trace.

*Yeah, right.* Both of them were far too proper for that, especially Ramsay, and besides, Ramsay left a lot of wealth behind. An elopement was about as likely as . . . as, well, Queen Elizabeth abdicating before Prince Charles turned sixty.

The words on the screen, already smeared and blurred to the point of illegibility, vanished into one long, gray smear.

She blinked back the tears, trying to focus on the stream of cases that had come before Ramsay. How on earth did she think she'd be able to tell which case had any bearing on his disappearance, and which did not? This was useless; she'd never find out what had happened to Ramsay and she would lose him forever.

Her head sank into her hands and hysteria bubbled in her throat, threatening to choke her. She tried to breathe normally, but the day's events were just too much. First Terrance and now this new frustration, this new pain.

For although she'd promised to help him win Lydia and to give them a happy-ever-after ending, what Jane wanted to do most of all was to hold Ramsay and keep him safe until the danger had passed.

But that would never, could never be.

It was a stupid, foolish thought.

The acknowledgment hurt.

She rewound the spool, fighting back tears. She could never tell Ramsay how she felt, never let it color her thoughts or actions, and definitely never show her jealousy that he had chosen Lydia.

She wasn't even in the running. She was too low-bred, not beautiful enough, not enough of a lady for Ramsay Chadwick. And she lived in completely the wrong time to boot. She'd heard of April–December romances, but this was more than a tad ridiculous.

She sniffed, a rueful twist to her lips. Enough of this goopy sentimentality. She had a goal.

She would do what she could for him, but first she'd have to get someone to translate the records into something a bit more legible.

She spent a fortune requesting copies be made for the months of August and September and agreed to pick them up the following day.

All she wanted to do now was eat some chocolate and curl up in bed.

# Chapter Eight

What a disaster!

Ramsay headed toward his temporary bedchamber, rubbing his slicked down hair into a rumpled mess. What had gone wrong?

It started out well enough. Mrs. Devereaux had at once assented to his plans for a private dinner with Lydia, assuring him he was still first in her daughter's heart, but he'd become wise to the sounds of worry and concern in her voice.

Lydia had at first delighted in the unconventional idea of eating on the floor. "You have an excellent housekeeper," she had said. "Why, it will be just like eating from the table."

He'd done all the right things: inquired after the events of her day, the latest gossip, and her planning for their upcoming nuptials.

She'd shared her thoughts on the first two willingly enough, but even he had noticed how she had stiffened into politeness on the matter of their marriage.

At that moment, they'd been helping themselves from the fondue pot. He'd gauged the time as being right for hand-feeding her.

He couldn't have been more wrong.

Leaning against the wall, Ramsay gazed across the hallway to his bedroom, the one where the ghostly Miss Leighton slept undisturbed. Even if she'd waited up for him, she'd be asleep now.

But perhaps they didn't need as much sleep in the future. Hopeful, he retraced his steps and opened her bedroom door just a crack. He peered in and found her indeed sleeping, her back to the door.

Tiptoeing into the room, he approached the bed. He wanted to tell her of the disastrous evening, and yet he didn't want to disturb her.

"I am haunting you," he whispered. "Wake up."

She shifted in her sleep. Would she wake? Triumph surged through him. Could he really reach her that easily? She rolled to face him.

His heart leapt into his throat. A large bruise clouded her ghostly upper arm. It hadn't been there a few nights ago. Rising anger threatened to throttle him. What had happened? Who had hurt her?

He swallowed. *Keep your temper, lad,* he told himself in an echo of his father's voice. Would that he were here now.

With infinite care, he lowered himself onto the bed, leaning over to see if she had any other bruises. There were shadows beneath her closed eyes, but she seemed otherwise unharmed.

That he could see.

He reached out to smooth her bruise. He refrained, his fingertips trembling with the effort. He wanted to comfort her, keep her safe, but she dreamed in her time and any protection he could offer was afforded only by the night.

He cursed himself for a fool. He was nothing to this Jane Leighton—a ghost, a figment of her imagination. She had her whole life in the future, her—what had she called it?—her career.

And even if it were possible, she was entirely unsuitable: a woman with no past, no family, no fortune. To even consider—

His back straightened. Of course he was not considering

any such thing. A little contretemps with his fiancée was no reason to run into another woman's arms. This was sympathy he felt, not . . . not a deeper need.

Even assuming she would want him.

His gaze fixed on her bruised arm.

Still, given half a chance, he'd kill the bastard that had hurt her.

He took one controlling breath and then another. He gazed down at her sleeping form. She looked innocent in her sleep, not at all like the wicked girl who teased him into a fury and then made him laugh again.

She slept. She surely would not wake . . .

His fingertips brushed her bruise, trailing further down her arm. The cold air grew warm beneath his touch, her skin turning pink.

She was here, with him. He withdrew his hand yet couldn't bring himself to leave her.

Her eyelids fluttered and opened. Her head tilted to look up at him. " 'Lo," she mumbled, still more asleep than awake. "How did dinner go?"

He almost hated to tell her he'd failed. "Not well."

That woke her up. She sat up, pushing her hair off her face. He itched to do it for her, to curl it around behind her ear. "What happened?"

He shuddered at the memory. "I missed and spilt cheese on her gown. She had a fit of the vapors and demanded to be taken home." He omitted the screaming temper tantrum, the broken plates, and the scars on his plastered walls.

Jane winced. "Ouch. I suppose stains are harder to get out in your time than in mine."

"I had not really thought about it." He knew he sounded cold, but he dared not display any other emotion. He wouldn't show the depth of his disappointment with Lydia and the failure of Jane's plan or the intangible feelings that now filled him for her. He wanted to protect her, that was all.

It meant nothing else.

Unbidden, his forefinger caressed her bruised arm. She jerked away from his touch. "What happened?" he asked softly, dangerously.

She shook her head, but her icy mask cracked. Her lower lip trembled. "Damn," she muttered in a most unladylike way, "I thought I was done with crying."

Her words jilted the cold into his heart, the chill of fear. "Jane?" A tear slipped down her cheek, and without even thinking, he brushed away the path with the pad of his thumb. "Jane?"

She flew into his arms, catching him unawares. "It was awful!" she sobbed. He felt awkward consoling the half-naked woman in his arms. He stroked her hair, the one part of her he felt safe touching. Why did she insist on wearing these flimsy, revealing garments to bed?

The heat of her skin came through the thin silky fabric, the soft mounds of her breasts pressing against him. He swallowed hard.

In a short while, she pulled back, sitting upright and wiping her wet cheeks. "I'm sorry," she murmured, her voice hoarse with tears. "I didn't mean to—" She sighed and pasted a strained smile on her face. "I don't want to talk about it. There's nothing you can do anyway."

His hands closed into fists. She didn't have to remind him of his impotence in that regard. "I can be your friend," he offered, "as you have been to me."

Her smile took on a rueful twist. "Some friend. My bad luck in relationships seems to have extended into destroying other people's. Yours, judging by tonight." She bit her lip for a moment.

He saw her mind ticking over and waited, relieved that her grief had abated. He never knew what to do when a female cried.

She spoke her thoughts aloud as she always seemed to do. "Perhaps if you bought her some expensive fabric to make a replacement gown? She might appreciate that."

"You won't quit trying, will you?" He smiled in relief that she seemed to be returning to her normal, unruly self.

This time her smile was genuine. "I don't think it's in my genes to give up."

"Geens?" He thought he'd become used to her baffling words and phrases, but she always managed to surprise him.

"A scientific discovery about a hundred and seventy years from now. It's how we inherit characteristics from our parents."

"Ah. Interesting." An intriguing concept. In fact, everything about her odd future life intrigued him. He didn't want to think of the reasons why. "Tell me more."

"I'm not sure how much you would understand," she began, grimacing in apology. "Darwin's discoveries haven't been written yet."

He smiled. The important thing was to keep her mind off her troubles—and his. "Try me."

She tried. He didn't think he understood half of what she said. A lot of it seemed arrant nonsense, and some of it sounded so commonsense that he was astonished nobody had thought of it before.

He took her hand in his, gazing at the scattering of freckles on the back of it. "So our bodies are made of cells unseen to the naked eye?" He raised her hand closer to his face. He thought he could perhaps make out light lines. Did they mark the boundaries of these cells? "And these cells contain the entire map to our appearance?"

"And some say the way we behave, although others argue that our upbringing and environment have more to do with that." She pulled her hand from his.

He headed back to safer ground, clasping his hands in his lap. He hadn't meant to get so close as to make her uncomfortable. He kept his voice even. "Incredible that maps so detailed could be so small . . ."

"It's complicated to describe. I only remember what I was taught in biology class."

"You studied biology?" Ramsay didn't know what to be more shocked by—that she had studied something so intimate and messy or that she had clearly advanced beyond most females in their learning.

She sighed. "You're not going to be impossibly male about this, are you?"

He didn't get the chance.

She read him a lecture on the equality of the sexes and how a woman could do virtually anything a man could do. His lips twitched, repressing a smile, and that alone got him a severe glare. How strange these modern ideas were.

"Think about it." She prodded him. How did she read him so well? "If women had more education and freedom today, their options would not be limited to governess, servant, or whore."

What she said made sense for women not in his class. "Not every woman can be protected by a man."

She beamed at him as if he'd made major progress. "Precisely."

Her response was so crisp and curt he divined she was one of those women she spoke of. Why else would she speak so passionately? Yet he couldn't help asking her, "And you, Jane? Are you one of these women who don't need protection?"

She rubbed her bruised arm and he silently cursed that he'd reminded her. He thought he saw sadness in her eyes, but it faded behind a forthright look. "Of course."

"Not even from that?" He gestured at the purpled mark on her white skin.

Her face twisted in pain. "A man caused it."

His fists balled up, but he sealed his emotions with a long-practiced mask. "What man? Are you safe from him now?"

She shrugged. "Terrance refuses to let go of me even though he already has a wife. Am I safe?" She shrugged again. "Probably not, but there is little I or the authorities can do about that."

Seeing her discomfort, he let the subject drop, allowing her to turn the conversation to a discussion of his current cases. She wanted to know their progress and whether anything new had occurred. He had never before spoken with a woman so intelligent and interested in how he spent his days.

Indeed, he had never spoken with a woman for such a long period of time without either one of them becoming bored. True, they occasionally had to explain unfamiliar terms or concepts to each other, but that was half the fun.

Half the fun. Incredible. A bone-stretching yawn put paid to further thoughts in that vein.

She rested a hand just above his knee. Didn't she know how intimate such a touch was? He focused on her words, willing away her touch. "You haven't had any sleep. You should rest."

He didn't want the evening to end and felt saddened that she did. "Tomorrow night," he said, "there is a private ball. You will dress appropriately and cover up that bruise. I don't want anyone to think I am the one beating you."

"As if anyone could think that," she retorted with a smile.

To his astonishment, she leaned forward and kissed him on the cheek. He smelt the softness of her perfume, of roses and something sweet. His eyes fluttered closed, inhaling her scent while she lingered by him.

"Thank you," she said, retreating at last.

"For what?" He had hardly rendered her any service. He'd not protected her from a violent man or, well, anything . . .

"For coming to see me tonight. For—for listening."

"You did not tell me much about your troubles."

"True, but having you here helped." She blushed at that.

He kissed her brow. It was the safest course of action. Any lower and he was in danger of capturing her mouth . . . "You are welcome. I only wish I could do more to repay you for all that you are doing for me."

She gazed up at him. "It will work out, Ramsay. It just has to."

Her words brought thoughts of Lydia, angry, screeching Lydia, to the fore. He winced. "Yes, it has to."

The words sounded hollow, even to him. Somehow, some way, he'd lost Lydia without even noticing. When had the pressing desire for Lydia vanished? Jane seemed to think her behavior tonight was excusable.

Murmuring a goodnight, he closed the bedroom door behind him.

He rubbed his brow. He was tired. That was all.

It was close to dawn already. They had talked for hours. If he didn't win Lydia back, he would lose her forever; and, if Jane were right, he would lose his own life as well.

To Ramsay's astonishment, Lydia visited him at his magisterial court. He wondered at her daring to enter the tavern alone and unescorted. He injected pleased surprise into his voice. "Lydia!—Miss Devereaux, what are you doing here?"

Had Jane's plan worked? Had his discussion with Lydia before disaster struck had some effect after all? His pleasure at her unexpected visit faded when he noticed a chairman's meaty paw clamped about her forearm.

This wasn't a willing visit. His voice sharpened. "Release her. What is the meaning of this?"

"She 'ad these, yer worship." The chairman flung a small handful of bank notes onto his desk. "An' she won't say where she got 'em."

"I will not!" Lydia declared, her spine stiff and her blue eyes fiery.

Struck anew by her beauty, Ramsay thought, *Truly, she is*

*a wonder, an Amazon, when righteously angered. Far more*
*appealing than that indulgent temper tantrum last night.*

He examined the bank notes. Forgeries, all of them. He
tried to sound reasonable. "But you must, my dear. It is un-
lawful to possess these fraudulent notes. You could be transported at the very least, hung at the worst."

"Fraudulent? Transported?" Her eyes widened in fear, but
none of her anger dissipated. "Do not call me 'my dear'," she
snapped. "You will not seduce the answers from me. As if you
were *ever* capable of that."

Her jibe plunged deep into his heart. What was she saying?
That he'd always been undesirable to her? The titterings from
the regular court-watchers brought him back to his senses. "The
room will be emptied now!" he boomed, pointing the way out.
The heat rose from under his cravat, burning his face. "Miss
Devereaux, Mr. Allsop, remain. The rest of you—OUT!"

He took a calming breath, then another, staring at the
grimy white-washed walls. Lydia was upset and frightened,
that was all. She didn't mean her words.

He wished for a cool cloth to dab his forehead and cheeks.
His heart pounded with unmerciful violence, denying him the
soothing satisfaction of his reasoning.

"Lydia, you must tell me everything." He kept his voice
calm and cool even though his mind raced. Could he avoid
charging her? It was impossible to imagine her fair loveliness
in a hellish prison or hung until dead. He swallowed. "How
can I keep you from the hulks if you do not?" Although his
fair skin had already betrayed him, he mustn't further hint at
how she'd hurt him.

He focused on her mulish, pretty chin while she considered
his request. To his relief, her shoulders sagged, the stubbornness
in her face replaced by uncertainty, fear, and apology. "Promise
me you will not be angry?" she pleaded.

"I promise." He made the vow out of hand. Nothing Lydia

could do would make him angry. Mortified, yes. He managed a tight smile.

"I won them last night."

"Won them?" Ramsay repeated, stunned. Lydia gambled? She'd offered no hint of this before. "Before or after . . ." He didn't want to remind her of their disastrous dinner.

She grimaced. "Afterward. I went home and changed out of my ruined gown—"

"Speaking of ruined . . ." Ramsay retrieved a brown paper package. "I bought you this in way of recompense for my clumsiness last night."

Lydia tore it open, revealing a bolt of emerald faille. "Oh, Mr. Chadwick!" she exclaimed, her eyes wide. "It's beautiful!" She held a length of the fabric to herself. "It will suit me marvelously, don't you think?"

"Most wonderfully," Ramsay agreed, beaming. His clerk, Mr. Allsop, coughed discreetly. "Getting back to what happened last night . . ."

Lydia wrapped the fabric in the remains of the brown paper. Her fingers lingered over the fine fabric. "I refused to stay in the house sulking, so I went to a party at Lady Westchester's. That's where I won it."

"From whom?"

Lydia hunched her elegant shoulders. "I cannot say. We were playing whist."

Mr. Allsop eyed the bank notes. "An unusual choice for a high stakes game."

Lydia directed a chilling glare at his clerk. Ramsay watched her face transform from disdain to the sweetest, most apologetic expression as she turned back to him. Her hypocrisy sickened him, a canker that surprised him with its vehemence. What was she trying to hide?

"Who played?" he asked.

"Myself, Lady Westchester, Mr. Wetherbourn, and Mr. Darby."

With Darby again? Ramsay frowned, forcing his mind back to the matter at hand. They were all people of impeccable fortunes and backgrounds.

Mr. Allsop must have read his mind. "Perhaps they received the bank notes from someone else and had not realized they were forged."

"Yes, that must be it!" Lydia instantly seized on the idea. "I did not know!"

"Leave it to us now, Miss Devereaux." Ramsay's thoughts were already bending toward the next step.

"What are you going to do?" She still sounded frightened, but for some reason, it didn't move him as it had before.

He examined her face. Was her fear sincere this time? "Question your partners and see where they might have picked them up." He remembered to turn his examination of her into a polite smile. "I will see you tonight?"

"Yes. Yes, of course." Lydia snatched up his gift and, muttering her goodbyes, left them alone.

Ramsay broke the silence that followed. "What do you think, Allsop?"

"I think we have a long day of cases ahead of us. Who do you want to assign the questioning to?"

"I will do it myself tonight. They are all guests at the Bartholomew ball." He waved his hand. "Let the others back in."


Jane returned to Chadwick's B&B, hardly noticing the graceful curve of the buildings and the blue sky above. A nice day for once. Despite the fine weather, she'd scurried out to pick up her requested copies of Ramsay's microfiched register from the library and hurried back again. She didn't feel safe on the streets anymore.

When she returned, she found Mrs. Marshall had visitors. "Oh, my dear!" trilled Mrs. Marshall. "Come in and see!"

Jane hovered by the stairwell, clutching her manila envelope of copies to her chest. "See what?"

"The ghost hunters have got some incredible recordings from your room last night."

"They did?" Intrigued, for she hadn't expected them to get anything, Jane entered the little sitting room. Ramsay Chadwick wasn't a real ghost after all. What could they have recorded?

Two scruffy, jeans-clad men, one about thirty, the other in his fifties, sat hunched over Mrs. Marshall's elegant reproduction Georgian sofa. Cooling cups of tea sat before them, ignored while they pored over concertinaed computer paper.

"This is Jane Leighton." Mrs. Marshall introduced her to the two absorbed scientists. When they didn't respond, she added, "The one currently sleeping in that room."

That caught their interest. "What did you see?" the older of the two asked, his beard pepper gray. His dark eyes keenly examined her.

She shrugged, wanting to make light of it. "Nothing unusual. He showed up much later than normal. Woke me up somehow. He was standing by the bed." No, that wasn't true; he had sat on the bed, but somehow that seemed too private to share.

"And then what happened?"

Before she answered, the younger of the two ghost hunters continued. "You see, there's this amazing spike of supernatural activity about here." He tapped the graph paper. "And then nothing."

Jane peered at the readout upside down. "Do you suppose that's when he disappears?"

"Is that what happened?"

No way would she tell them the truth. Time travel in a Regency bedroom? She'd never see Ramsay again, and he would be plagued with historians, scientists, and tourists.

She shrugged casually. "It was just a suggestion." Before they asked her more unanswerable questions, she tapped the envelope tucked under her arm. "I have research of my own to do. If there isn't anything else?"

"No, no, not at this time. We'll be recording again tonight, Miss Leighton. This spike could be a fault of the equipment. I hope you don't mind."

She managed a smile. "No, not at all. I'll be very interested to see the results."

*Not.*

She escaped the ghost hunters and retreated to her room upstairs. She'd half a mind to unplug all their equipment, but they'd realize she'd done so and would want to know why.

She sighed. So long as she kept her mouth shut, nothing bad would happen.

Right?

Besides, Mrs. Marshall would get her haunting rating and not conduct an exorcism of her room. Even though she knew he wasn't a ghost, she didn't want to risk losing him. Not while there was still a chance she could help.


Dressed in all her Regency finery, Jane rubbed her eyes. The photocopies were even harder to read than the documents were on the microfiche reader, but she had managed to work out some of the words.

She wanted to show it to Ramsay and get his help, but a new danger might lurk there. Reading cases that hadn't happened would bring him knowledge of his future and all that she had read of time travel stated that this was a very bad thing.

The sun had set an hour ago, and she'd been waiting for him to arrive. The door handle rattled.

She glanced up from the photocopies, surprised by the noise. Ramsay's entrances were usually silent. The door opened, and the white figure of a boy entered. He looked no more than ten years old, and he was dressed in ragged clothes.

He stared at her, seeing her sitting on the bed. He could see her! And she could see him! How strange. She'd never seen anyone else but Ramsay before. Was this another who needed her help? Or was it a younger version of Ramsay himself?

The boy's jaw gaped and he let out a silent yell. He turned to flee, fading from sight.

Jane set aside the photocopies on the bed, gnawing at her lip. Would this be the only ghostly occurrence she would see tonight? Would Ramsay still be able to—

Ah, but there he was, impeccably dressed in his black and white evening attire, striding toward the bed.

He unceremoniously hauled her to her feet, making the connection a natural, every day occurrence. His abrupt release of her hand made her stumble a step back toward the bed.

"Was that you?" she gasped. "The boy?"

He shook his head. "That was Billy. He should not have been in the house, let alone my bedroom. You gave him quite a scare if his screaming is anything to go by."

"That would be punishment enough, I would hope," she said, feeling sorry for the boy.

His "quite" chilled the air. "Show me your bruise."

Partly hidden from one end by a puffed sleeve and from the other by her long gloves, modern make-up concealed the rest of it. "Amazing," he murmured, not even touching her.

He straightened, seeming to recollect some notion of propriety, the polite mask falling into place again. "Are you ready, Miss Leighton?"

"Of course." She accepted his hand and frowned at him. Something had happened to cause this new distance. "You called me Jane last night."

His cool mask cracked. "It was . . . different last night."

How could it be different while they held hands like . . .
like lovers? She slipped her hand from his grasp.

He escorted her from his bedchamber. "We must put on our
public faces and our public manners."

She frowned at him. "But we're not in public."

"We soon will be."

"Really, you can be such a bore." Jane stomped down the
stairs behind him. She sounded spoiled, she knew, but she
couldn't help it. The new distance between them hurt more
than she'd expected.

He paused halfway down the first set of stairs, looking up
at her. "A bore? Is that what you really think of me?"

His frozen expression, its suppressed pain, stabbed her in
the heart. "Of course not, Ramsay—Mr. Chadwick," she hastened to reassure him, reaching him but not daring to touch
him again. "Would I be helping you win Lydia if you were?"

"Much good that it does," he grumbled, resuming his
downward progress. "I am much more at ease with you, Miss
Leighton, than I ever am with Lydia Devereaux."

His words alternately warmed and alarmed her. "But you
love her," she protested, following him down the stairs, past
the landing. "Why is it so difficult?"

"It is her beauty." He didn't look back at her, seemingly
lost in a reverie. "I lose all shreds of conversation when I be-
hold her."

"Thanks a lot!" Jane wished she had something to swing at
him. She hadn't wanted *that* comparison.

He glanced back at her from only a few steps ahead. "Forgive me, Miss Leighton, you are lovely, but—"

"Sometimes, Mr. Chadwick, you can be an idiot." She stormed
by him, nodding at the butler as he opened the door for her.

Men! No wonder she'd been having an uphill battle with
Lydia.

# Chapter Nine

By the time Ramsay entered the carriage, scowling, Jane
had repented her sharp words. "I'm sorry, Ramsay. That was
rude and unfair of me."

Fortunately, he accepted her apology without demanding
further explanations. Even so, for the remainder of their jour-
ney, a chill remained in the air.

They arrived at Lady Bartholomew's. Ramsay gave her little chance to drool over the beautiful house on Laura Place,
limiting her one moment of wonder to the staircase as they
ascended to the ballroom. She wished her little flat had
painted cornices like that. They looked like they came right
out of a Wedgwood catalog, the white painted swags of green-
ery standing out in the warm candlelight.

Ramsay gravitated toward the Devereaux party. Lydia's
barely polite smile sent the room's temperature plummet-
ing even further, but her mother almost fell over herself
greeting them.

Nevertheless, Jane received a sharp-edged smile from the
older woman. Jane guessed the woman did not entirely trust
her because of her continued absences during the day.

Before Ramsay even had a chance to speak, Lydia sent him

off for a glass of cordial. His worried gaze met with Jane's. Their mutual concern banished their last argument. So long as they fought the same battle, their tentative friendship remained secure.

She shrugged helplessly at him. What could she do?

Ramsay gave a reluctant bow, inching away until it benefited him to move with rapidity in order to hasten his return.

Jane glanced at Lydia. Already the blonde's demeanor had improved. Jane watched her smile gaily at the assemblage, scanning those present and murmuring catty remarks back to her mother.

Lydia looked so carefree, so happy, so ignorant of what her future held. *Perhaps if I warned her about her death,* Jane thought. *Then she'd take more care.* But the words wouldn't come. How could she possibly explain how she knew? Her strange behavior already had her on the borderline of being dismissed from Society—and she couldn't be ejected yet, not without making sure both Lydia and Ramsay were safe.

Jane admired the women's costumes and the pretty chandelier before remembering that she had a greater purpose in being there.

She sought to find a topic with which to engage Lydia in conversation. "I am sorry your tête-à-tête with Mr. Chadwick did not go well last night."

Lydia opened her mouth to answer, the happy light going from her eyes, but her mother beat her to it. "Miss Leighton, I was surprised not to find you in last night. Where were you?"

Her heart pounded with consternation. Ramsay hadn't explained? "Mr. Chadwick did not say?" she asked, buying time.

The sharp, reproving line of Mrs. Devereaux's mouth softened. "Mr. Chadwick was too caught up in my daughter to pay much attention to my questions. Nobody on staff would answer either."

"Mr. Chadwick prides himself on his discreet staff. In his line of business, he has to."

"Business!" Mrs. Devereaux snorted in disgust. "Mr. Chadwick is a gentleman pursuing . . . gentlemanly pursuits. The magistracy is not a business."

Oops. "I stand corrected."

"Why would the staff need to be discreet about you, Miss Leighton?" Mrs. Devereaux's fan rustled with anger beneath her beetled brows. "Now, my girl, you will tell me where you were."

She'd run out of time. Jane pasted on a smile and dipped into her Austen repertoire. "I went down to the Westwood Buildings. I have an old friend who resides there. I brought her a basket and we had a very pleasant, quiet evening."

Lydia's mother relaxed. "You are a kind girl. Forgive me for my suspicions."

"Suspicions?" Jane strove to look surprised, pleased she had landed on the right excuse. *Thank you, Miss Austen.* "Why, I suppose my headaches have made me look rather strange. It's the light, you see. Sometimes it feels like it stabs me in the eyes."

Mrs. Devereaux hemmed solicitously. "What do you take for it?"

"Nothing works except rest and darkness." Jane sighed, hoping she wasn't overdoing it.

"I'll have my physician send something around. I had those terrible megrims when Lydia was younger. Awful." Mrs. Devereaux patted her arm. "We'll soon have you out and about."

Jane somehow managed to smile, wondering when Ramsay would return and rescue her from this awkward conversation. "Thank you, Mrs. Devereaux. You are too kind."

"And Lydia did well out of her little contretemps with her fiancé last night," Mrs. Devereaux continued. "She brought home the finest bolt of fabric I have ever seen. We sent it off to be made into a gown, didn't we, my dear?"

Lydia's attention had wandered. Jane felt a touch annoyed to be beneath Lydia's notice, but then she remembered she was the poor cousin after all.

Lydia made a startled half-turn back to them. "Oh, yes. It was the most beautiful emerald color, like the deepest forest, so rich and yet so light. It feels so soft too. I can hardly wait to wear it!"

"Sounds lovely," Jane murmured, her fingers itching to examine the cloth already. "I look forward to seeing you in it. I'm glad it all turned out well in the end."

"He is a man," relented Lydia. "He cannot help being clumsy, I suppose. But then there are very graceful men . . ." She trailed off. Jane traced her adoring gaze and winced.

Darby. Of course *he* would be graceful.

He joined their party, and before either of Lydia's companions could raise a mild protest, he whisked her off into a waltz.

Jane tracked their swirling path: the delight in Lydia's face and the way they held each other (too close!) all suggested disaster. She hoped the waltz would end before Ramsay retur—

She stared, struck by Ramsay's frozen form on the edge of the crowd. He held two gleaming glasses of cordial in his hands. Only his eyes moved in his otherwise immobile face.

She didn't need to trace the direction of his gaze to know who he followed. The lines about his eyes and mouth tightened. He shot a glance at her, speaking volumes. Did anyone else see and understand that look of anguish and betrayal?

Abruptly, he turned and disappeared into the crowd.

Shortly after, the waltz ended, and Darby returned Lydia to them. He nodded briefly at the three women before leaving them without a backward glance.

"Lydia, a waltz?" Mrs. Devereaux reprimanded under her breath. "Have you any idea of the scandal?"

Lydia flipped open her fan and waved it idly, dispelling the flush from her cheeks. "We've waltzed before, Mother. Mr. Darby will stand up with Mr. Chadwick at the wedding. Where is the scandal in that?" She made a face and snapped shut her fan. "Where is he?"

"Mr. Chadwick?" Jane shrugged as if she didn't care. As if she didn't want to hike up her skirts and run after the poor man. "Perhaps you ought to find him."

"What an excellent idea!" Mrs. Devereaux enthused, smiling upon Jane for the suggestion. "I will come with you. Will you manage by yourself, Miss Leighton?"

"Of course," Jane reassured her. It looked like Mrs. Devereaux didn't trust Lydia and Jane didn't blame her. The girl didn't seem eager to see Ramsay again.

Rather than be stranded against the wall, she circled the room, drifting by elegantly dressed men and women watching the dancers on the floor. She wanted to join them and take time to revel in the Regency world firsthand, but Ramsay's absence concerned her. Had he left?

Through a doorway leading into the supper room, she spotted Mr. Darby taking his leave of Ramsay with parting glares on both sides. He was still here, much to her relief, and he had no doubt just taken Mr. Darby to task for his bad behavior.

Mr. Darby spotted her at once and approached. She watched Ramsay disappear in another direction without a backward look. "Miss Leighton," he greeted her with a brief bow, constrained by the sheer number of guests. He didn't appear too discommoded by Ramsay's words. "You have cut loose from all your ties? Where is the fine Lydia?" He scanned the room for her.

"Looking for her fiancé, I expect," Jane replied.

Her words didn't seem to have a dampening effect upon him. "Pity." His lips twisted into a half-grin.

"Isn't it?" she returned tartly.

His expression sharpened. "Miss Leighton, may I ask what your interest is in this little affair?"

"Whose affair are we talking about, Mr. Darby?" While he stood there gobsmacked, she realized they should continue the conversation where they wouldn't be overheard.

She couldn't lead him outside. She'd read enough Regency romances to know that would be an unforgivably forward thing to do. Her only other choice then was the dance floor. She didn't want to add to the gossip mill. She glanced at the steps. A cotillion: she could do that without thinking, almost. "Mr. Darby, would you care to dance?"

Mr. Darby's jaw dropped further. "Miss—Miss Leighton, a young lady does not—"

Jane blew out air from the corner of her mouth in a sharp, impatient huff. "Mr. Darby, as you just suggested that I might not be a lady, being cut loose from all ties, what does it matter?"

Her recovered, his dark brow quirking in interest. "Are you not?"

"I am bored," she lied glibly. "If nobody asks me to dance, why should I base my happiness on a man's whim?" She extended her hand. "Shall we?"

A wolfish grin crossed Darby's face. He accepted her hand and led her to the floor. "Does Mr. Chadwick know about this?"

"Know about what?"

"That he has a forward hussy ensconced under his roof?"

Jane laughed softly. "Really, Mr. Darby, you can be quite insulting."

He led her into a turn. "Forgive me, my dear, but I had assumed we would be frank with each other." His gaze dropped down to her bosom even as she twirled away.

"Very well, let us be frank." She twisted to fix him with her sharp gaze. "What are your intentions with Miss Devereaux?"

"Intentions? Should there be any intentions?"

Her eyes narrowed. The other dancers were not that close

nor that interested to bear their conversation any attention. Why did he delay? "Mr. Darby, haven't we just agreed to be frank?"

"But we haven't agreed to keep each other's secrets . . ."

"I don't have any secrets," she bluffed.

"No?" Darby grinned. "Perhaps you could explain why Chadwick's bedchamber, the one you've commandeered, is empty."

Swallowing, she ignored the warning thuds of her heart. "Because I am here dancing with you." She delivered a creditable smile.

He ignored her childish response, leering with a strange eagerness. "I have it on the best authority that the room is inhabited by nobody but ghosts. I think the question here should be: what game are you and Chadwick playing at?"

"Ghosts?" She managed a shaky laugh. How had he learned that? And after Mrs. Devereaux had told her of the staff's discreet loyalty! "That's hardly a reliable source."

"You didn't answer my question."

She smirked at him. She couldn't show him her fear of being unmasked and rendered useless. "You never answered mine."

As they stepped in a close circle, an arm about each other, he murmured, "Shall we vow that we will keep each other's secrets?" He leaned closer, his breath wafting past her ear.

Alarmed, Jane glanced sidelong at him, wondering how to answer. Darby seemed to be suggesting more than a simple promise of silence. Not that she could give it anyway. That would mean betraying Ramsay. And she would never do that.

She almost wished the glittering chandelier above them would be so obliging as to give her one of her fictional headaches.

Thankfully, the next dance step drew her out of his embrace, but she did not relish his return, for she would have to answer him then.

* * *

After speaking with Darby, Ramsay needed a drink. Even though Darby had convinced him of his innocence in the bank note forgeries, Ramsay still had a bad taste in his mouth.

He'd barely managed to refrain from yet again questioning his friend's motives in dancing—and so intimately!—with Lydia. Just the sight of them together wrenched and twisted him. He knew Darby would only laugh and treat his questions as a jest, making him feel worse than he did now.

Best to leave that alone.

He took a glass of claret from a passing servant carrying a gilt tray. The alcohol warmed his throat, the pleasant autumnal fire at distinct odds with the fears and jealousies roiling in his mind.

Under the veneer of polite social chatter, he'd interrogated all but one of Lydia's whist partners. None of them knew anything about the forged notes. He preferred not to speculate, but things weren't looking good for the fourth member of Lydia's whist game. Yet he would wait for all of the evidence before making a judgment.

He ascended the stairs back to the ballroom, taking his time. He needed to think. He bumped shoulders with guests moving downstairs to play cards in relative peace, letting their murmured apologies wash over him.

If Jane—Miss Leighton—was correct, this could be the case that spared he and Lydia from a lifetime of heartache—or even allowed them to live a lifetime. If Lydia was betraying him and further, was truly participating in a capital crime, he would have that lifetime of heartache anyway, and his Jane would not be able to help him. As he could do nothing to help her.

*His Jane.* He snorted at the fanciful notion. Jane Leighton could no more be his than he hers. What was the best they could hope for if the worst came to pass with Lydia? Snatched nights of passion and dull days apart. That was no life.

He swallowed, pulling his mind back onto the proper path. Had he become as fickle as his Lydia? Lydia *was, is, and would be* his, soon to be sealed in the sight of God and the law.

His thoughts consuming him, he almost walked right by Lydia until her mother's mild coughing fit brought him back to his senses.

They stood on the landing outside the ballroom. He glimpsed dancers through the crowded arched doorway. He returned his attention to the Devereauxs.

"My apologies, Mrs. Devereaux, Miss Devereaux." He bowed to the two women. "I did not see you." Did Lydia look miffed at his negligence? His hopes rose. Perhaps Jane was right and Lydia flirted to make him jealous, more romantic. He was tired of guessing. He had to know for sure, but how to find it out?

Where *was* Jane? Why had the Devereaux women left her to mingle alone? He craned his neck to look for her in the ballroom, but he was unable to catch a glimpse of her.

"We have been looking for you," Mrs. Devereaux said.

He ignored the mother and focused on Lydia, his mind burning with only one thought. Perhaps all he needed to do was ask to get his answer. He'd find Jane later and hope she hadn't disgraced herself in the meantime. "Miss Devereaux, may I speak with you in private?"

Lydia's eyelashes fluttered in modest decorum. "Of course."

Tucking her arm into his, he led her upstairs. They turned off the landing and into a wide hallway. The doors were closed on either side, so he gestured she sit on the window seat at the end of the hallway. Below, he saw the winking streetlights of the city and the stream of steady traffic along Great Pulteney Street.

He would have preferred a room, but this seemed the only place where they would not be interrupted.

"You know your way around very well, Mr. Chadwick," Lydia remarked, disengaging herself and sitting down, putting distance between them now that they were alone.

He didn't like that. She should welcome him, not . . . He closed the gap, sitting beside her. On the edge of the window seat, she had no further room to retreat from him, her soon-to-be husband. He began by explaining his familiarity with the house. "Lady Bartholomew is an old friend of the family, but you knew that." He took a deep breath. Now that he had her alone, he didn't quite know what to do with her. "Lydia," he murmured.

She must've seen something odd in his expression, for her eyes widened and she leaned away. Why would she be afraid of him?

He kept his voice calm, soothing. Cool. "Lydia, there is something I need to know."

"I told you," Lydia said in a deep voice of barely controlled emotion. "I do not know where those forged bank notes came from."

"Blast the blasted bank notes!" Ramsay's control shot wide in search of his patience. He struggled to recover, feeling his face warm. "Lydia, it is about our—our engagement. You have not been happy of late. If there is a chance for you to be happy, my dear, I will gladly set you free."

The expression of hope that washed over her face dashed his insides to painful shards. He pressed a hand against his side to keep the agony within. She didn't love him.

A sweet, pleasing mask concealed the devastating hope. "I thought you loved me."

He opened his mouth to answer but the words wouldn't come. "I . . . You are the most beautiful woman in Bath and I would be honored to have you to wife." He couldn't believe he continued down this dreadful, blighted path, but some-thing, some need, pushed him onward to speak the words, to ask the question that would sunder her from him. "But if you would not be happy, then do not feel obliged . . . I am not sure if you love me."

Pushing her away hurt him. It hurt him all the more to see how willingly she would go.

She took a breath to answer and halted, her mouth a small 'o'. When she spoke, her voice sounded cooler than the autumn mist. "Mr. Chadwick, you and I have made a contract to be wed, and we will be bound by it. I will be honest. I do not love you. I can not, will not ever love you, but I will marry you."

His mind reeling, he hardly fathomed her last words. "You still wish to marry me?"

"It is a good match," she said, her face expressionless. "Arranged marriages worked for our parents; it may well work for us."

His parents had married for love. It had not been arranged. The remembrance leapt unbidden into his mind. He gazed at Lydia: she seemed empty, devoid of life. Certainly, she held no love for him; she had confessed as much. And yet she still wanted to marry him.

It hurt even to breathe. He closed his eyes, blocking out the shadowy corridor, trying to block out the sounds of gaiety ris-ing from downstairs.

He had to ask, even though he knew the answer. He searched her face for some trace of the love he was sure she must've felt for him once. "Do you love someone else?"

Lydia's brittle laughter gave him the answer. "Love! Why all this talk about love? Love is to woo and win. Love is for play. It isn't for life."

Frozen, Ramsay watched her rise and saunter away from him. "I could end the engagement." Why should he let him-self be cuckolded, and by his best friend, no doubt? Why should he marry without hope of even contentment with his choice of wife?

She spun, her blue eyes snapping with anger. "With our wedding four days away? I would sue you for breach of promise. This match *will* happen. If you jilt me now, I will be ruined for life."

"I think you are overstating the matter—" he stuttered, stunned by her harsh words. This was no childish tantrum, but cold, heartless anger.

"I do not overstate." She snapped her fan open, furiously fanning herself. She halted and shut her fan, her mask in place again. "It is done, Mr. Chadwick; let it be done. We can have our own fun if this 'love' you want does not come to us in time."

Her degenerate declarations made him sick to the stomach. And trapped. He couldn't end the engagement now without an excellent reason. Not without destroying Lydia's life and she didn't deserve that just because she didn't love him.

He needed to think. He needed to talk to Jane.

He rose, delivering a curt bow, the perfect gentleman. He felt as if a savage tore him up from inside. "Good evening then, Miss Devereaux."

Unable to think above the roar of blood in his head, he stumbled down the hallway, brushing past her and heading for the stairs.

How could he be trapped with Lydia? Trapped? Why did he see it that way? Just days ago, he would've thrilled to hear her affirm she would marry him and to hell with all the rest.

His feet fell heavy on the steps down to the ballroom. Her beauty would have been enough for him once. He'd have had the courage and conviction to believe that she would come to love him, for hadn't she been attracted to him in the first place, at least sufficiently for her to agree to the wedding?

It was for the money. He knew this in the pit of his stomach.

With his greater fortune, he had purchased the Devereaux's pedigree, albeit half-French. A man rising out of the merchant class should be grateful for such a match.

The words had a familiar echo. Had he overheard them somewhere before?

He entered the ballroom, seeking for Jane with an odd desperation. Jane, he could talk to. She would understand.

Where was she? She hadn't been with the Devereauxs. Had she gotten into trouble? He saw her on the dance floor and relief submerged beneath incredulity.

Her arm was about Mark Darby's waist, her head close to his dark, bowed one. Mark whispered something to her and she smiled, *smiled,* back at him.

His brain threatened to explode. Did Mark intend to steal everyone he cared about? Her caustic comments on their way out this evening rushed back into his memory.

*No.* He couldn't bear it. Not for another moment.

Still promenading in their intimate embrace, they passed him on the edge of the crowd. They didn't see him.

Without even thinking, he reached out and grabbed her wrist, hauling her out of her graceful position. She yelped. He glared at her. "We're leaving. Now."

When he put his mind to it, Jane thought, Mark Darby could be quite amusing. As they stepped into the allemande, arms interlocking, she kept her distance.

Her other arm gracefully extended to the side, she focused on moving through the steps. She wished with all her might that the dance would end.

He drew her closer. "Am I that unpleasant?"

She glanced at him, finding him too close for comfort. He'd let her lack of an answer from his challenge slide, but she knew he would bring it up again. She managed a smile. "Of course not."

"I find that difficult to believe. Prove it." His dark eyes sparked, daring her.

She could see how a younger, more naive miss would fall for this roguish charm, but to her it felt . . . greasy. "A gentleman wouldn't ask a lady to prove something. He'd take it on faith."

"What unusual ideas you have about gentlemen." He squeezed her waist. "And what ever made you think I was one of that number?"

Refusing to show her fear, she smiled at him, wishing for something to jab him with. She didn't want Ramsay to have to deal with another scandal that was her fault.

Someone yanked hard on her free arm, catapulting her out of Darby's arms. She yelped with surprise. The hand gripping her wrist so tightly belonged to Ramsay.

"We are leaving," he growled. "Now." One look at his reddened face, and Jane knew some disaster had struck. What had Lydia done now?

Without a word of protest, she let him usher her from the ballroom, down the L-shaped staircase, and out of the Bartholomew house. He must have forewarned his coachman before collecting her, for the carriage was ready and waiting for them.

Ramsay helped her inside and followed close behind. With a sharp jerk, the carriage moved off.

Jane glanced sidelong at him. His fists lay clenched on his thighs. "What happened?" she murmured, not daring to, but wishing she could touch him. Lydia must've done something terrible this time.

"What happened?" His chilly voice deepened, grinding out the words. "What happened?" He turned and grabbed her by the upper arms and shook her. "Why don't you tell me what happened?"

His grip dug into her arms, causing fresh pain to her bruises. She cried out, trying to push him away, her fists pummeling his implacable waistcoat.

"Tell me. Tell me!" he demanded, his face mottled red and purple with his anger's strength.

"Let me go! Ramsay, for God's sake, let me go!" Tears filled her eyes. He was just like all the other men in her life. She refused to tolerate violence from any of them.

It was over. Their non-relationship was over.

Instantly, he freed her, his gloved hands rising as a kind of barrier between them.

Her frightened sobs became uncontrollable, but she didn't care. She'd pack her bags, go back to London, and have a chat with Terrance's wife. If that didn't keep him away, well, maybe she'd just sell up and emigrate.

She twisted away from him, burying her face against the side of the carriage. It rocked awfully, but it felt safer than facing Ramsay right now.

"I—I—" She heard him stutter above her wracking sobs, all his anger disappeared. "Jane . . . Jane, I am . . . I am sorry." She felt the feather-light touch of his hands on her shoulders. She froze, keeping very still. They brushed her once, twice, hovering, uncertain.

"Jane." He sounded miserable, but she'd heard the pity line before too. "Jane, I never meant to hurt you. You know I would never hurt anyone . . ."

She didn't know that. She had seen him control his anger, the fiery anger so many redheads seemed prone to. She raised her head from the squabs only to wipe the tear trails from her cheeks. She still couldn't bear to look at him.

His hands moved away from her shoulders. He spoke quietly, brokenly. "Jane, I have not lost my temper like that in years, I swear it. Forgive me, Jane. Forgive me, please."

Her mind raced, reviewing what had happened. He hadn't actually hit her, just shaken her, like a man driven to the edge of his wits. It had not been so violent really, nor would it have hurt if she hadn't already been bruised. If she hadn't suffered that attack from Terrance, would she have reacted in the way she just had?

She had believed in Ramsay, trusted in him all along, why should that change now?

It didn't excuse his actions but it was unlike him. If he ever hit her . . . By God, if he hit her, he wouldn't know what hit him.

She shifted, twisting back to face him. His pale face was filled with contrition. "You—you frightened me," she admitted with a slight stammer. She rubbed her sore arm.

"Your arm," he groaned. "I forgot. Jane, I swear—" He held out his arms in contrition and she flew into them. They closed about her, warm and comforting, with none of the repressed violence that had been present just moments earlier.

The tears rose again and she sobbed against his black coat. "After Terrance . . . I couldn't bear it if you were . . ."

He let her cry. It felt so good, leaning against him, like she had never leaned upon anyone before.

At length, he gently pried her loose. "Jane, I am not like that." His gloved thumb smoothed over her wet cheeks. "I am an ape, an idiot, a fool, but not a bully, Jane. Never a bully. I have a temper but I've not lost it since I was a boy." He grimaced. "Not until tonight. Forgive me?"

She believed him. The agony writ over his features, the consternation in his eyes. The remorse and the guilt. She stroked his cheek. "Ramsay . . ."

"Never again, Jane," he murmured, his voice husky. "I swear it. I know there is nothing I can do to convince you of that . . ."

"Ramsay . . . You shook me, that is all. After Terrance . . ."

She took a deep breath. "Even the smallest act of force would scare me. I overreacted."

"So did I." He stroked her cheek, perusing her face, searching for her forgiveness. She managed a watery smile, certain she looked horrid after all those tears.

The distance between them shrank into nothing and his mouth was on hers. His lips felt warm, right. Instinctively, she knew he sought reassurance, as she did, that everything was okay between them.

She returned his kiss, her mouth opening slightly beneath his, beckoning, but he didn't take up her invitation.

Instead, he pulled back, his lips parted. His chest heaved with deep, unsteady breaths. So did hers, for that matter. His fingers trembled as he briefly touched his lips. "That—that should not have happened . . ."

His raw-voiced statement punctured the growing warmth she felt within, but she rallied. "It's only a kiss between friends," she told him, managing a shaky smile. "It happens frequently in my time when one needs comfort and reassurance."

"A kiss like that?" He sounded as breathless as a debutante.

She had to be honest. "No, not all friend kisses are like that—" She took a steadying breath. None of them were, if she were totally honest. She changed the subject, desperate to get his—and her—mind off the kiss. "What did I do to make you so mad?"

He winced at the reminder. "You and Darby . . ."

"I danced with him only to get information." Jane cut him off, trying to ignore her heart's lurch of happiness. Ramsay was jealous? Did their kiss mean something after all? It couldn't—He couldn't—*Focus, Jane, focus.* "All I got was charming double-talk. He is adept at avoiding questions."

He frowned. Didn't he believe her? "Thinking upon it now, I believe he dodged a few of mine as well."

"It's not surprising," Jane continued, settling back, putting a little distance between the two of them. She could kiss him again if he only looked at her a certain way. Instead, he seemed to be lost in some abstract problem.

"How does this not surprise you?"

"If he does not want us to find out how deep his attachment to Lydia runs, he will not tell us, short of torture."

Ramsay shuddered elegantly. "They do that in your time?"

"No civilized country does," Jane told him, although she wouldn't mind putting Terrance on the rack. He sunk into his deep thinking. "Ramsay, that can't have been the only reason you were mad at me. Did something else happen?"

He shot her a startled gaze, stumbling over words in his haste to agree. "Of course not. Nothing happened. We are just friends, after all. One dance with Darby—" He halted his babbling and looked down at his hands.

He spoke so softly, she strained to hear it. "I spoke with Lydia."

"And?" She watched him curl inside himself even though he didn't move a hair, the old barriers rising. This couldn't be good.

He shook his head. "I cannot talk about it. Not now. Not even to you."

# Chapter Ten

Ramsay shook his head, trying to get his muddled thoughts in order. He still couldn't believe that he'd behaved so child-ishly, in so ungentlemanly a fashion toward Jane. What had he been thinking? His method of removing her from the Bartholomew household would cause talk, if not scandal.

And now the one reason he'd come in search of her—to discuss his disastrous conversation with Lydia—and he found himself speechless. Jane confused him, and his actions to-ward her confused him more.

No, he couldn't talk to her about Lydia. At least not tonight. He wanted to talk to her about it, about what Lydia had said, and get a woman's opinion on the matter, but he couldn't ask her about that now.

Not after he had kissed her.

He rubbed his pursed lips, turning to stare out at the lamp-lit blackness beyond. They were almost home. Soon she would be back in her own time, and then he could think clearly about what he needed to do. He had managed without her before. He could figure this one out too.

"It was that bad?" Jane had withdrawn to her side of the

carriage. So it had occurred to her too that their kiss had been improper. After all, they now spoke of his fiancée.

He caught her wary gaze. "She still wants to marry me."

She winced and attempted to hide it beneath a smile, but he'd become surprisingly adept at reading women lately. He wished he'd had the skill before. "That doesn't sound bad."

Her jollying tones grated. "She does not love me."

He hadn't meant to tell her, but there it was, out in the open. His marriage was destined to be a loveless one, and there was nothing he could do about it.

Her voice came to him, soft as moonlight. "Ramsay . . . I don't know what to say . . ."

A silence extended between them, broken only by their arrival at his home, where he gave quiet instructions to his footman and his butler. He escorted her inside and to his study.

He should take her to his bedchamber and bid her goodnight. Yet here was where he felt most in control and he needed every iota of control he had if he was going to make it through the night with his honor intact.

He stood behind his high-backed chair, the expanse of his cherry wood desk between them. Safer that way. "Miss Leighton," he began sternly, drawing her attention to him. For some reason, the dark blue walls and bookcases had distracted her. "It seems to me that whatever the cause of mine and Lydia's disappearances, it has naught to do with our impending marriage—and if it does, then our fates are sealed."

She appeared shaken, her hands twisting as she paced before him, wearing a groove in a Persian carpet already ancient when his father had bought it. He wished she would stop but knew not how to ask it. "Your fates are not sealed," she protested. "They cannot be. Why would I be here otherwise?"

He didn't want to think of alternate reasons for her presence. In spite of everything, the memory of her lips haunted him. He had to purge himself of that.

She stopped and faced him, her eyes filled with a desperate hope. "Perhaps I have done it already. Your engagement was on the verge of disintegration. Now that it is back in order—"

"You do not understand, Miss Leighton," he interrupted her coldly. "The wedding was never off. You have not changed a thing—except make me aware of the . . ." He paused, searching for the right word. "The inadequacy of the arrangement. I would have gone to the altar gladly, believing I was loved, if not for you."

She flinched as if he'd slapped her. "I—I'm sorry." She ducked her head.

"What do you suggest now?" She had to see there was nothing left for her to do here, no reason to come back.

Except maybe to love him, and that was out of the question.

Her hands stilled, clenched, and then relaxed. "I suggest, Mr. Chadwick, that you go far away, very far away until the date of disappearance has passed."

"Jilt Lydia at the altar?" Abandoning his honor like that horrified him. How could she even suggest it?

Her gaze begged him to listen. "Perhaps some business has taken you away unexpectedly. Tell her before you go that the wedding is not off, only delayed. You want your union to be unblemished and happy, do you not?"

His lips twisted, mirroring her own sarcastic expression. "That is all that is left to be done? Run away?"

She stood silent before him.

"No." He circled around the desk. "I will not run away. I will not be a coward." Unable to stop himself, he brushed her cheek with his hand, his voice gentling. "You have fore-warned me, Miss Leighton. I will be armed and ready for whoever attacks Lydia and I on that fateful night. Whatever happens will happen."

Her eyes glittered. "It does not have to be that way."

"It will not be that way, Jane," he murmured. He moved

away, burying the tenderness he felt for this modern woman. It was time to send her back.

When he turned to tell her so, she had gone.

Jane lay on her bed—Ramsay's bed—her eyes squeezed shut. She didn't want to see any more of Bath's Regency period. She didn't want to be reminded of Ramsay just by looking about his room. Little touches of him were everywhere: the shaving mirror and basin, the legal handbooks at the side of his bed.

She had ruined another relationship. She'd seen the hurt on Ramsay's face, heard it in his voice. She'd come in and wrecked his life as if it had been her own.

After that kiss, that stupid, idiotic, breathtaking kiss, she'd felt distrust build its barrier between them. By that single, unthinking act, she'd killed their friendship too.

Even a simple friendship with a man appeared beyond her grasp.

*Idiot. Fool.*

Why did she seem hell-bent on destroying everyone she cared about? She groaned, recalling all she had done. The intimate dinner, the quiet moments together, everything could be seen, could be conspired to be seen, as a jealous rival set on destroying his attachment to Lydia.

It had worked too. She hadn't meant for it to happen like that. She'd buried her attraction to the man. There was no future in loving a man some two hundred years dead. She'd fought always to do what was best for him, to make him happy with his choice in mate.

His misery tonight, tightly reined in but there, had been too much. It was all her fault. She shouldn't have meddled. She should have focused on his court cases, not his love life.

She didn't blame him for hating her.

Covering her eyes with her arm, Jane let out a convulsive sob and longed for dawn to take her away.

Ramsay paused outside the door, his hand hovering above the handle. He'd been surprised when she'd fled the room. He had not thought her the type to run, but to always stand her ground. How could anyone be afraid if they had the temerity and courage to step into and live in another lifetime?

Had their kiss disturbed her more than she had admitted? He had pushed her away, establishing boundaries he'd somehow never bothered to set before. He had rejected her, reduced her worth to him. He was betrothed to another. He had to remember that.

He pressed his ear against the door. At first, he heard nothing. Perhaps the wood was too thick to transmit sound. A gasping, wrenching sob muffled by the dense wood was soon followed by another.

He had hurt her. His fingers tightened about the doorknob, but he held back. He could not obey his instincts and go to her. It would undo everything he had said, level every wall he had started to build since Lydia had given him the horrible news.

There was to be no love in his life. He should not be seeking it with Miss Leighton. He winced. He should not have kissed her.

A boy's voice piped up. "Mr. Chadwick, are you afraid?"

"Billy." Ramsay identified the voice as belonging to a mop of dirty blond hair and a dirtier face beneath it pressed to the stair railings as if they could hide him. "Afraid of what?" Could the child read his mind?

"The ghost in your room, sir. Is that why you sleep somewhere else now?"

Ramsay frowned. The boy had picked up too much too soon. "There is no ghost."

The boy shook his head firmly. "I saw it wiv me own eyes. She looked like Miss Leighton. Is Miss Leighton a ghost, a demon, a devil-woman?"

Ramsay discovered he had taken a protective stance in front of the door and self-consciously moved a few paces away. "You have an active imagination, child. Miss Leighton is not a ghost. Perhaps we should have your vision checked."

The boy stood on the penultimate stair, his hands on his hips. "I saw right through her!"

What could he tell the boy? The truth? It was no more fanciful than Billy's ghost tale, but could his silence be trusted? "Billy, my boy, can I trust you to keep a secret?"

Eyes wary, the boy nodded.

He decided to play on the boy's superstition. "Miss Leighton is no ghost. She is a . . . an angel. She told me that Miss Lydia and I are in danger of losing our lives, and she's here to help us avoid that."

"Then why does she look like a ghost?"

Ramsay thought hard and quick. "You cannot see angels during the daytime, Billy. The sun is too bright. It is only at nighttime that you can see them. You must have seen her as she was gaining her substance."

"And she's not a ghost? Or a demon?"

The boy seemed convinced. "Neither. She is innocent and seeks only to help." Ramsay rested a hand on the boy's shoulder. He should have talked to him before this. "I only tell you this, Billy, so you won't be afraid of her. I do not want to hear this pass from your lips. Miss Leighton, for all intents and purposes, is my cousin and so she must stay if she is to succeed in saving my life. Do you understand?"

"Yes, sir." The boy's vigorous nod had no effect on his

tousled hair. "I'd protect your life wiv me own after all ye've done for me and me brothers."

Ramsay's cheeks warmed. "Yes . . . ahem . . . well," he muttered, feeling a bit guilty for spinning the boy such a Banbury tale. "Now, you must to bed for you'll be up soon enough."

Billy shrugged. "It's almost dawn. I should be up anyway. Night, Mr. Chadwick, you can trust me."

Ramsay almost missed the boy's last words, turning back to his bedchamber door in a sudden, blind panic. *Almost dawn?* He bolted across the narrow hallway and flung open the door.

Jane lay in abject misery, curled up in a ball. The first of the morning light glimmered through the window and she faded away like the mist, gone before he could even say a word of apology or to comfort her.

He swallowed.

"Cor . . ." sounded an awed Billy from behind him.

Struggling to contain his tangled emotions, Ramsay snapped, "William, go."

He heard the boy's light footsteps dash downstairs.

Ramsay sighed. He supposed it was for the best.


Jane stumbled downstairs just before the window of opportunity for breakfast closed. She'd showered and washed her face thoroughly, scrubbing away all signs of tears, all signs of yet another failure.

Five tables in total crammed into what had been Ramsay's study. She idly wondered what had happened to his books. All fallen apart with age by now, no doubt.

The ghost hunters sat at a table nearby. Jane ignored them and blearily read the breakfast menu. Something hot and greasy and incredibly bad for her health sounded like just the ticket.

Mrs. Marshall's eyes widened as Jane gave her order. "No muesli?"

"Not today. I want to treat myself." Jane managed a smile. "I'm on holiday, aren't I?"

"Of course, dear." Mrs. Marshall nodded and went back into the kitchen.

The older of the two ghost hunters joined her. "Miss Leighton," he began. Jane shot a look at him. He sounded just like Ramsay.

He looked nothing like him, however, with his rounded, gray-bearded features, dark where Ramsay had been pale. His dark brown gaze widened momentarily at her startled expression. "Would you prefer it if I called you Jane?"

She nodded.

"All right, Jane, forgive me for asking this, but early this morning, our sound recorders picked up the faint sound of . . ." The researcher looked embarrassed. "Of crying. Was that the ghost?"

Dumbly, Jane shook her head.

"Did the ghost make you cry?"

Somehow, she managed a shaky laugh. Ramsay had made her cry but not in his ghostly attire. "No, not really." She fixed a polite smile to her face. "You might have heard that I was attacked recently. I think it was just . . . stress from that."

The ghost hunter nodded. "Good, we can rule out that recording then."

*What? No sympathy? Thanks a lot.*

The ghost hunter continued, "The sharp psychic spike occurred again last night at a different time." He consulted his notes, scrawled on a small notepad. "At about 10:43 P.M. Was the ghost in your room then?"

Jane nodded, not trusting herself to speak.

"What I want to do is be sure that this spike isn't caused by your psychic energy."

That made her laugh. "I don't have an iota of psychic energy in my body! That's ridiculous!"

"So you think," the ghost hunter continued intently, "but you are the first to have repeated visits from this ghost. I would like to check the room without you in it. Mrs. Marshall has a vacancy and—"

"You want me to move out?" Jane stared at him, horrified. She couldn't move out. Ramsay needed her! She chewed on her lower lip. No, he didn't need her anymore. She'd done enough damage.

"For just one night, Jane. I can understand the attraction and excitement of sleeping in a haunted room. This way too, we'll be able to use our infrared video cameras to pick up any images. With you there, we have not been able to, naturally."

"Naturally," Jane echoed. Ramsay could live without her for one night and she could do with a night of solid, unbroken sleep. "Very well. I'll switch rooms for the night." She'd take a nap and then get back to work on the deciphering the register. It was useless now, of course, but she wasn't ready to let go, not yet.

Ramsay counted the hours, even the minutes until sunset. He wanted to apologize to her. He had practiced his speech for much of the afternoon in between settling cases.

The apology was only for being so harsh with her, for initiating a kiss that should never have happened. She was a practical girl from the future. She would understand, once her feminine emotions had settled, that all he had said was right and true. He'd made an error in the manner of telling her. He had not wanted to hurt her.

Would she forgive him?

He unlocked the door to his bedchamber, pocketing the key, and entered at the moment night fell.

Lighting a lamp, he gazed in consternation at the bed's smooth counterpane. Where was she?

He crossed to sit in his accustomed place by the fire. He'd never arrived at sunset before. Perhaps he was too early. Did they keep different hours in the future?

He waited.

He crossed to the built-in bookshelf and plucked a volume at random. Retreating to his comfortable wing-back chair, he lit a lamp with a taper and settled down to wait for her.

Jane let herself into the Chadwick B&B. She'd eaten at *The Golden Friar,* a posh restaurant on Laura Place. It amused her that she'd partied there the night before, two hundred years ago. The decor had gone gilt, more Victorian than Georgian or Regency, but the food remained exquisite. This trip was hurting her credit card balance, but until last night, it had been well worth it.

She unlocked the door to her temporary room. The irony of it struck her, and she smiled wryly. Two hundred years ago, Ramsay would be sleeping in this room because she'd taken over his bedchamber.

Best that she not be there tonight for him to reach out and bring her back to him. She'd made a more than sufficient mess of matters, and it hadn't changed a thing. All the histories remained the same. He and Lydia would vanish, die, in less than three days.

She hadn't made a spot of difference. She curled up on her bed, flicking through the photocopied pages of Ramsay's magistrate register.

His words still taunted her, his wounded expression, the cold shell, the tenderness and sympathy he'd shown her in the end. He had resigned himself to his fate; she saw it in his eyes, and she didn't know if she could ever make him want to live again.

She had to admit it: it would be a long night without him.


Ramsay shut his book with an angry snap. Where was she? Why hadn't she come? He'd been waiting for hours. Had that man, Terrance, captured her and prevented her from coming to him?

He tossed the book on the floor. He glared at it and then stooped to pick it up, placing it back in its rightful place on the shelf. He stared at the shelves for a long moment, not seeing them.

He had not really dared to think the worst. That she had chosen not to come back. That she had taken his hint and had left him to his own devices.

This night, then, would be his first taste of all the nights to come. Alone and without her.

He turned at the sound of Trenby's cough. His valet gave a brief bow. "Mr. Darby is below to see you, sir."

Ramsay's brow creased. "At this hour?" He nodded. "I'll see him."

He rose, crossing to the shaving mirror to tidy his cravat.

Darby was waiting for him in the study. Ramsay stiffened further. This was the last place he'd seen Jane, if he didn't count her fading form on his bed. It made his mood even more sour.

"What do you want, Darby?" he growled. He strode to his desk, his gaze raking across its surface. Nothing had been moved or changed. When had he stopped trusting Darby?

"In a bit of a bad mood, dear boy?" Darby piped cheerily. "Did I interrupt something?"

"Just some reading."

"And where is the delicious Miss Leighton?"

Ramsay didn't like the way he used the word 'delicious' or said the word 'Miss' as if it were a slur. "I would ask you would not refer to her in that way."

Darby took his ease in one of the wing chairs by the fire. "Which way is that? You object to her being referred to as delicious or being a miss?"

"Miss Leighton is not in. She's—she's visiting a friend." He rested his arm on the back of the other wing chair. Darby hadn't come to talk about Jane, surely.

Darby's eyebrows rose. "She has more than one 'friend', does she? Very magnanimous of you."

Ramsay remained still, very still, certain that if he moved, Darby would find himself on the floor. "I thought we were friends, but you're talking all in riddles. What are you speaking of?"

"What half the town of Bath is already wondering about— is Jane Leighton your mistress?"

Ramsay choked.

Darby grinned. "No, thought not. You don't seem the sort to have that in you. Pity though, she's a sweet thing and oddly loyal to you, but I suppose you *are* the rich relation . . ."

"Yes, I expect that is it." Ramsay willed his heart to calm down.

"Of course, she's very forward for a country lass. If I didn't believe you, old man, I'd think she had more than a touch of the Town bronze on her. More than a touch."

Ramsay sighed. "I'm sure you didn't come here tonight to talk to me about Ja—Miss Leighton."

"But I did. Had to warn the groom about the gossip. If this doesn't give Lydia an excuse to cry off."

"She won't cry off." His words were clipped. "I thank you for the warning, but I am sure you will reassure everyone that Miss Leighton has an impeccable reputation."

"And that we'll see her at the wedding as a family

representative?" Darby's smile grew wolfish. "I should trust your word, Chadwick, but I'm sure you'll understand if I ask for some recompense for telling your Banbury tale. For," he continued, "I know she's not your distant cousin or any such relation as sure as I'm sitting here before you."

Ramsay barely heard him, fury pounding at his ears. "You want me to *pay* you?"

Darby rose, his hands risen to keep Ramsay at bay. "Forget it. It is clear you are in no mood for a joke. Don't worry, your secret is safe with me." He tapped the side of his nose and saw himself out before Ramsay could react coherently.

He had to put a stop to that rumor, otherwise Mrs. Devereaux might think twice about allowing her daughter to wed him.

He sat down. Perhaps that wouldn't be such a bad idea.


Shaking with a sick fury, Jane sat on the bed waiting for him. More than ever, she was glad she'd taken a night off. That one night had been enough to reveal how little he'd helped her all along.

*How could he? How could he? Bloody men.*

Her bathroom door opened and Ramsay strode through, dressed in shirtsleeves and with bare feet. He stopped, arrested by the sight of her.

*Bet he never thought he'd see me again.* She scowled at him. She felt foolish dressed in her Regency finery, but she wasn't about to let him get on with getting himself killed before she'd given him a piece of her mind.

He gestured to someone unseen behind him and then walked toward her, his hand extended, his face bland and polite. Couldn't he read the anger on her face?

*Ha, he'll regret bringing me back into the past this time.*

His hand slid into hers and turned into warm human flesh.

She jerked her hand free. "How dare you? How *dare* you?" She itched to slap him.

He stared down at her. "How dare I what? I apologize if my words from last time upset you but—"

"Upset me?" She surged to her feet and planted the point of her finger into his chest. "Why didn't you tell me Lydia was arrested?"

His brow furrowed. "You did not need to know. I was investigating the matter and—"

"I didn't need to know?" Jane echoed, astonished. "We have this damn connection—"

"Language!"

"This *damn* connection," she repeated, her mouth twisting sourly, "and you have the gall to say I didn't need to know? You could have put me to work—to find out if the forgery had any bearings on what happens to you, but no-o-o-o."

She expected him to yell and rant back at her. A full-blown, screaming match was just what they needed in her opinion. Where was his redheaded temper now?

His cheeks reddened. "Have you finished?" he asked, dropping to a mild whisper, grating it out between gritted teeth. "If you are finished yelling, this conversation is at an end."

He walked away, crossing to a bureau against the wall and fumbling with his shirt cuffs. Tension radiated from him.

She stared after him. "What if I'm not done yelling?"

He continued to fumble with his cuff, half-turned away from her and scowling. "It isn't going to make you feel any better. In my experience, it always makes one feel worse." Something bounced from his fingers onto the rug and rolled with a dull clink to the dark floorboards. "Damn."

"Let me." Gathering her skirts, she crouched and retrieved the small button. Rising, she handed it to him, not daring to look up at him. She reflected upon her harsh words. She'd gained nothing but temporary karmic satisfaction. Nothing more.

"I'm sorry," she murmured. "I know you don't want me to help you anymore, but I regretted the missed opportunity." She helped him with his other cuff. "It could've meant the difference between your life and death."

He casually dropped the button onto the mantel. "Did you find anything?" he asked, his voice vibrant with a hint of hope and something more that Jane didn't want to decipher.

She shot him a shrewd glance. "Not yet. The handwriting is difficult to read. I have not learned anything that rules out the forgeries as the source of—" She trailed off. She'd mentioned death once too often this evening.

Ramsay sat in a wing-backed chair by the fireplace, the same one she had slept in all those nights before, pulling on his stockings. Jane glanced away, caught up in a centuries-old thought that she shouldn't look at his bare calves.

She shouldn't look anyway. He belonged to another.

His calm, conversational tone reinforced that belief. "I will tell you what I have learned on the way."

"On the way where?"

He took his coat from the wooden form that held it and shrugged it on. "To Sydney Gardens. There are fireworks tonight."

"You want me to come?" After what she had done? Why? She couldn't believe it.

He rose, stockinged and shod, and crossed to her. He gathered up her hands in his. Without gloves (she'd forgotten hers in her anger), his warm hands felt smooth, soft. "Of course. Jane, I was angry and . . . and upset. I said things I should not have."

Jane whispered, "They were true, but I never meant—"

"Hush." His fingertip brushed her lips. "We must be on our way. We are meeting the Devereauxs for supper."

Unable to help it, Jane grimaced and was shocked to find its echo in Ramsay's face. Yet she said nothing. What could she say that wouldn't be construed as wanting him by her and away from Lydia? For that's what she wanted to do to keep him safe.

"It must be done," he explained. "Although the joy in it has gone, I will marry Lydia. I am sure this sounds all very archaic to you, but one does not always marry for love. We will beget the heir and spare and live our lives as separately as possible."

"That's awful," she murmured.

"Not so awful really." He smiled thinly. "My life will not be much different than it is now. Once our fates are defeated, as they will be. Are you ready?"

"I left my gloves—"

He retrieved a pair from the bureau drawer. "You left these behind the first night."

She struggled with pulling them on as they descended the stairs, trying not to put a special meaning to the fact he'd kept them. "What did you mean that your life will not be much different?"

He helped her into the carriage. "I will not betray my vow to Lydia once it is made. There will be no mistresses or any other to steal my heart. My heart is apparently not worth stealing."

In the darkness lit only by the carriage lamps, his profile lay in shadow. He turned to her, his eyes glittering briefly. "Jane, how fortunate I am that I can tell you these things. I dare not speak of them to anyone else." She caught the curve of his lip. "What a shame you cannot stay in this time. You would make a fine companion."

"You do not know me," Jane contradicted. "Haven't I already proven to be a disaster? I have turned your world upside down. Ruined any happiness you might have had."

"Yes, but it is better to know. And at least it's been fun, for the most part."

She goggled at him. "Fun? You enjoy my mistakes?"

A glint of teeth hinted at his wry smile. "No, I enjoy seeing my world through your eyes. You are refreshing, Jane."

"Like a long tall glass of water," she remarked dryly, secretly flattered. At his puzzled look, she laughed. "Never mind, Ramsay, it's modern slang. Now, tell me about these forgeries . . ."

They discussed his meager findings in the case, the possible leads. It washed all the barriers away. They conversed easily once more. Jane offered, "I will talk to Lydia. Perhaps she'll mention something she was too embarrassed to mention to her betrothed."

"That would be tricky without letting on how you found out about it."

She smiled. "I'll think of something."

"Be careful."

Her smile grew into a grin. "I'm not the one in danger. You are, remember?"

# Chapter Eleven

Ramsay assisted Jane from the carriage. They stood at the entrance to Sydney Gardens with its wrought iron gates that framed a stately hotel set back from the road by a graveled drive. Many lamps and sconces lit up the broad, graveled path into the Gardens proper, casting a ruddy, golden hue upon the arriving guests.

"It's beautiful," Jane breathed. "Like a fairyland." For once she didn't miss electric or fluorescent lights.

She glanced at Ramsay to find him beaming with pleasure. "This is one of my favorite places in all of Bath. Although technically, it is in Bathwick."

She smiled. He would be technically correct.

She remembered their carriage crossing the unseen Avon and had peered out to look at all the dimly lit shops lining the Great Pulteney Bridge. That was the old border, she supposed.

She shot a sidelong look at him as they promenaded along the drive's slight incline. She didn't have the heart to tell him that forty years from now, the railway would sunder Sydney Gardens in two.

He seemed to have read her thoughts. "What is this place like in your time?"

"It's not quite so large," she dodged the truth, "and it has been overshadowed by a large park and botanical gardens to the southwest of the Royal Crescent."

"A pity," he murmured and she squeezed his arm.

"Remember," she soothed, "there are about two hundred years between now and then. Do we have time to tour the whole park before supper?"

His lips twitched ruefully. "We must at least pay our respects to the Devereauxs, else they will think we have abandoned them. After supper, there will be time enough for a tour. It is the best time to see the illuminations."

"Illuminations? What are they?"

"There's one over there." They had walked along a corridor radiating from the hotel and had stepped into the park proper. She leaned into him, looking over to see a large sheet hanging from the back of the hotel. A shadow image of a seventeenth-century woman and a bowing man was projected onto the sheet.

"Pretty." She pulled away from him, too aware of their closeness. She surveyed the evening scene. The corridors had emptied into an open space lined with booths, each having their own table and enough space to seat six or even eight. Almost all the tables were taken.

She heard the faint strains of strings and wondered where the orchestra was hidden. Perhaps around the next bend . . .

"You truly did not know of the illuminations?"

Her attention drawn back to him, she shook her head.

He grinned. "Then I shall enjoy showing more to you." The pleasure died from his voice. "Ah, there they are."

The Devereaux women had commandeered an entire booth to themselves. Neither woman rose at their approach. "Mr. Chadwick, you're late," Lydia reproved, glaring sharply at them.

"It is my fault," Jane said hastily.

"The delay was my fault," Ramsay said at the same time. They exchanged an amused glance. She made a slight gesture to let him take the lead. "My day at court ran overlong," he said, "on a case you are familiar with." He directed a meaningful look at Lydia and Jane saw her flush.

"Let's not talk of business," Jane said, sitting at the table. "Miss Devereaux, how are the wedding details progressing?" It was the last thing she wanted to hear about, not the least because such things had never particularly interested her, but she was hobbled by her nighttime visitations to this era. What *did* young ladies talk about?

Lydia's response seemed even less enthusiastic, so Jane steered the conversation to Lydia's gown, exclaiming at its lace.

"It's locally made," she pouted. "I wanted foreign lace, such as Brussels, but it is so hard to come by these days."

"You cannot tell," Jane returned, managing to sound sympathetic. "The work is very fine."

The conversation struggled throughout supper. Jane grew aware of the poisonous glances directed to her from Lydia and her mother. Ramsay noticed them too and fell into a troubled silence, sending only an apologetic look her way.

How long would this freezing out continue? Jane had had enough. She laid down her silver-toned fork. "I am a plain-spoken woman from the country. Will not one of you say what is on your minds?"

"It does not surprise me that one of your sort is plain speaking." Lydia shot a look at her mother before returning to pick at her plate, head bowed.

"One of my sort?"

Mrs. Devereaux took a sip of wine from a cut-glass goblet. "Miss Leighton, it has not failed to come to our attention that you are a peculiar creature. Your migraines hit you with surprising frequency and short duration. We only see you in the evening."

"I never thought," Lydia's head tilted toward Ramsay, her

voice choked, "that you would flaunt your mistress so in front of me!"

"Mistress!?" Jane shot a glance at Ramsay. He'd paled, his lips clenched as if to retrieve the word he had spoken in chorus with her. Pain flickered over his face before his mask came crashing down, concealing all emotion.

Lydia looked at her and then him. "I knew it! And you talked to me of love!" She leapt to her feet and ran into the night.

Ramsay half-rose from his chair to go after her.

"Leave her," Mrs. Devereaux ordered with quiet steel. "You have done quite enough damage."

"There must be some mistake," Jane said, struggling to make amends. Was it at all possible for her to destroy Ramsay's life any further? She shot a heartfelt look of apology at him. "I am his cousin, not his mistress."

"You are not his cousin." Mrs. Devereaux fixed her with an eagle eye. "There have been rumors, and so I have had you investigated. I had sympathy with you at first, but when I found out you share Mr. Chadwick's bedchamber . . ."

"Billy," Ramsay muttered under his breath. "Damn Darby." Only Jane sitting by him heard it.

"I do not share it," Jane responded to Mrs. Devereaux's accusation, calmer now. "He gave it up to me. It has a quieter aspect than any of the other guest rooms. It helps my headaches." Jane saw no point in indulging in hysterics, but she had to clear up this misconception before it left Ramsay's marriage in shambles.

"What Miss Leighton says is true," Ramsay interjected, "and her honor should not be so impugned. By repeating this, Mrs. Devereaux, you destroy her prospects."

"If you wish it," Jane said quietly, "I can move on to my next destination."

She heard his breath hiss inward.

Mrs. Devereaux beamed, not at all disconcerted by the idea

of Jane leaving. "My Lydia is upset, of course, but she under-
stands the married life and that she need only be faithful to you
until the requisite heir and spare are produced."

He winced and Jane flinched in sympathy.

"If you were using this woman to get you off the hook, it
will not work. The marriage will happen as planned." Mrs.
Devereaux's eyes narrowed, her mouth pinched. "We are not
so rich and we have invested a great deal into Lydia's
trousseau to make her worthy of your station. I believe I could
bring a breach of promise against—"

"Madam!" Ramsay interrupted, his pale face now red.
"You have said enough. I am well aware of my duty. Nothing
can terminate this marriage contract unless Lydia herself
breaks the agreement through word or action."

Jane rose, finding her legs a little shaky. "We should find
her. She should not wander about the park alone."

Mrs. Devereaux followed suit. "Is that how you 'fell,' Miss
Leighton?"

Biting back a retort that her "fall" had occurred in an ex-
clusive London hotel after too much champagne, Jane turned
her back on the rude woman. She threaded her way through
the tables, taking the direction Lydia had fled. Behind her, she
heard Ramsay inquire about Lydia.

He caught up. "The labyrinth."

"A maze?" She shot a worried look at him, the light dim-
ming as they walked away from the blazing pavilion.

"Don't worry. I know the way like the back of my hand. I
have traversed it many times." His strained smile made her want
to kick Mrs. Devereaux who trailed behind. "It helps me think."
His voice lowered further. "I am sorry about the Devereauxs's
accusations. I had heard the rumors too but had ignored them.
I didn't know if you would be back. I should have thought,
should have protected you more."

"Oh, that's all right." She waved him off airily. "I've heard worse."

"That doesn't make it hurt any less." His arm slipped through hers and she gave it a grateful squeeze.

They plunged into the tall green hedges of the labyrinth, shadowy and ill lit. The festivities were directed elsewhere this night.

Yet quite a few had sought the labyrinth's shelter from prying eyes. Jane glanced up at the darkened posts in the center of the maze, backlit by the golden glow of lamps. They looked like they had baskets hung from the two upper ends. "What are they?"

He looked up. "It's the merlin's swing. When you get into the center, you can be hoisted up above the maze and direct, or misdirect, people."

"What a shame it's not working tonight." She gazed upward at the structure, so forbidding in the dark. "Someone could point out Lydia for us."

They hurried onward, Ramsay releasing her arm only to grasp her hand. He may have feared that she'd be left behind like Mrs. Devereaux, who lagged increasingly, her stertorous breaths sounding behind them. His hand gripped hers tightly, the warmth seeping through their gloves. She couldn't pretend it was a casual hold, but she squeezed his hand in silent reassurance. What more could it mean, after all?

"What did Lydia mean that you had spoken to her about love?"

"She sounded upset to you?"

"She sounded like a prima donna to me," Jane replied sharply before she'd thought. "Sorry. It did sound more like a sneer."

"It was at the Bartholomew ball where I asked her if she loved me . . ."

She squeezed his hand again. "You need not say anymore."

They passed a couple ambling slowly, arm in arm. "Excuse me," Ramsay asked, "have you seen Miss Devereaux?"

The gentleman nodded and pointed ahead.

Jane reflected it was fortunate that Lydia was the most beautiful girl in Bath and thus well-known, for each person they passed had seen her and pointed the way.

"Not all that helpful, considering we're in a maze." She spoke her misgiving aloud.

"But I know the way through."

"Does Lydia?"

"Of course. She's lived here for much of her life, like myself. Neither of us need a map."

Jane got the sudden sense that Ramsay had loved her for almost as long. "But if she does not want to be found, won't she take one of the dead ends?"

She heard his sharp intake of breath. He sounded affronted. "An unmarried woman would never venture into one of the false paths alone."

"I may not know much about etiquette in this time, but she shouldn't have run off into the maze alone either."

"Why do you think we're here?" he said in a tight voice.

She fell silent, a hundred reasons running through her mind. To see that she's safe, to make apologies, to make sure the marriage was still on, to woo her back . . . Jane buried her dislike of the last idea.

They reached the center of the labyrinth. Couples flitted about the perimeter, arm in arm. The green hedges seemed a popular romantic hideaway. None had seen Lydia.

She looked back the way they had come. "Then she must have made a wrong turn."

He followed suit. "She was upset," he mused.

"Yes. She's probably behind us now, or she's walked back out the way she came."

Mrs. Devereaux emerged from the narrow path to find them approaching her. "You cannot be giving up on my daughter!"

"On the contrary, Mrs. Devereaux," Ramsay replied smoothly. "She has not come this far. We are returning to look for her."

Their combined presence attracted some attention, not the least because Ramsay had asked every person about Lydia's whereabouts.

His face reddened, partly concealed by the darkness, the scattered lamps in the maze providing little light. His mouth tightened to a dark line, leaving Jane feeling helpless in his wake.

They plunged back into the maze, slower this time, and Mrs. Devereaux kept up with them.

As did half a dozen couples curious to see the outcome. The cavalcade wound its way back through the maze, gathering others along the way. Jane heard the whispering gossipers behind them, as each party they passed caught up with the salacious theories and joined the procession.

She wondered if any of them thought it was odd that Ramsay Chadwick's supposed mistress had joined in this search for his fiancée.

They searched one wrong turning after another, the crowd hanging back to see if they returned before pressing forward.

Not all the young lovers had been content to take a secluded stroll. Rustling in the bushes warned of couples amorously entwined. To Jane's amusement, Ramsay bid her to stay behind while he went ahead to investigate a dead end occupied by a pair of lovers.

"I do not know why you try and spare Miss Leighton's feelings," Mrs. Devereaux said at last, huffing for breath. "The harlot has probably seen more than you."

Chuckles, gasps, and outright laughter sounded behind the stout matron.

"Very true, Mrs. Devereaux," Jane replied coolly. She had

nothing to gain or lose in this era by admitting her experience. All she needed was to see Ramsay past his fated death and into a new life, and she would leave Regency Bath behind for good. "But at least Mr. Chadwick is gentleman enough to think I may have such sensibilities."

They retraced their steps to the main path. Ramsay's grip was tight on her arm. "How experienced are you?" he murmured in her ear.

And she'd thought it hadn't mattered. Of course it did. To him. "In my time, I'd only be considered a harlot by the most puritanical." She glanced sidelong at him. He waited for more information. "What do you want to know?" she flung back at him, suddenly defensive.

"Forgive me, I did not mean to be intrusive."

She snorted and relented. What did it matter now? "I had three lovers and all, I thought, were committed long-term relationships at the time. Satisfied?"

"Three?" The knowledge sounded like it strangled him.

"Think of me as a widow," she advised, hating the disgust in his voice and wanting it gone. "It would be a fair parallel. I am a respected businesswoman in my time and my personal life is of little consequence."

The longer she stayed in this era, the more she picked up the language. The sooner she got back, the better. Her staff in London mightn't be able to understand her if she kept this up. But she didn't want to hurt Ramsay anymore—or be hurt by him.

"I see." He paused at a right turning. He added in a voice most of their followers heard. "This way almost gets you to the center of the labyrinth." By Jane's estimation, they were halfway back to the entrance.

"It would be an easy mistake to make," Jane murmured, stepping closer to him. She didn't like the press of people behind them. They reminded her of dogs who'd caught the scent of prey. Jane hoped they would give up and leave them alone.

Yet she knew that hope was in vain.

They took the wrong turn, hearing conversation and argument spring up behind them. After a few minutes, the crunch of gravel warned them that some, at least, had chosen to follow.

Their path twisted and turned, the sounds of lovemaking and impassioned sighs becoming distinctly more audible, sometimes fading as they made a turn. The sounds didn't all come from the same couple, and Jane didn't know whether to be relieved that there wasn't one highly active couple or that there were so many.

"This is the last turn before the dead end," Ramsay muttered. Rustling and soft cries hinted that a couple occupied the terminus, although they could be on the other side of the hedge.

"Let me." Jane squeezed his hand. He returned the squeeze and she glanced up at him, the lamplight deepening the tense lines on his face.

She wanted Lydia not to be there, wanted her waiting for them back at the supper tables, wanted this agony over for him. She stepped around the corner.

A couple lay partly buried against the thick leafy hedge. The man's breeches crumpled around his knees, his hips concealed by the woman's legs and the skirt of her diaphanous gown.

A gown that Jane had praised earlier in the evening.

"No," she breathed, stepping back. She pressed her palms against Ramsay's chest. "No."

"I begin to think you have been boasting emptily." He sounded amused by her dismay. His lips twisted into a bitter smile. "You need not protect me."

"Just take my word for it and let us go home." She tugged on his arm, wanting him away from the untold hurt that lay just beyond his sight.

"Home?" He gazed down at her, his eyes narrowing.

She'd said the wrong word. Damn. "Please, Ramsay . . ."

He pushed past her and strode into the dead end. "Lydia!" The cry wrung from him grated with pain. His rising fists clenched and unclenched.

Jane reached for him, but he shook her off. She stumbled back. Nobody else should see this either, but she couldn't hold back this many people.

"Damn you, Lydia Devereaux!" he roared. His bellow brought the last of the laggards hastening forward. Pressed against Ramsay, it seemed impossible to Jane that any more people could fit in the small space. She gripped his hips and eased herself to one side of him. She didn't let him go. He had to know he wasn't alone in this. He had to.

Mrs. Devereaux stood silent, aghast. There were no words for her daughter's actions. Lydia was ruined.

Lydia's glazed expression focused, and she buried her lover's head against her bosom, wanting to conceal him. She sneered at him. "If you can have fun with your little piece of skirt, why cannot I?"

Her lover struggled free of her suffocating embrace. He hitched up his breeches, straightening to face the man he'd cuckolded. "Sorry, old man." Mark Darby grimaced in a rare, genuine apology. "What man could refuse such an offer?"

Lydia's laugh tinkled above the shocked silence.

"The wedding is off," Ramsay grated. Jane felt him vibrate with restraint. "I will not acknowledge either of you again. You are both dead to me."

He whirled and shoved his way through the crowd. Jane followed in his wake, wishing again that they weren't the entertainment of the night.

Once past the crowd, he turned on her. "As for you, Miss Leighton, this is your fault!"

She dodged his accusing finger. "My fault?" she echoed. "How is it my fault? I didn't put the two of them together!"

He about-faced, heading for the labyrinth's exit. She

followed, not wanting to get lost in the dark green corridors. "The first night I saw you, those two were in an embrace barely more decent than—" He pointed behind him, his hand shaking.

"You're not being logical," she accused, picking up her skirts so she could keep up with his long-legged strides. "I had nothing to do with that and you know it!"

He stalked on, and silence fell between them, a silence unpricked by the rising bubble of gossip they left behind, the music from the orchestra, or the angry screams of Lydia.

What could she say or do to help him now? She gentled her tone, placating. "Ramsay, I'm sorry. If I could have prevented this, I—"

"You drove her into his arms!" he roared.

"I—what?" Dumbfounded, she stopped in her tracks.

He gesticulated wildly. "Tonight, you all but confessed to being my doxy when you are no such thing, and you drove her into his arms! I bet Darby has been waiting for this to happen."

Jane hastily reviewed the supper conversation in her mind. "I said no such thing. It was Lydia and her mother who—"

"No excuses!" They broke free of the labyrinth, and he strode down the slight slope toward the hotel and the gates.

She hurried after him. "Ramsay—"

"No!" His face was almost purple with fury. "You've done enough. You've done more than enough. I never want to see you again. Do you hear me? You have ruined my life! It might as well end now."

Stunned, Jane watched him stride toward the wrought iron gates, his fists clenched at his sides. She wanted to cure him of his hurt but she wasn't wanted now. She never had been. How stupid of her to think otherwise.

Behind her, the fireworks roared into joyous life, transforming the night sky into a profusion of red and gold bursts.

It was over.

* * *

Shivering and sniffling, Jane knocked on the front door of Chadwick's B&B. Spending the entire night out-of-doors hadn't been at all pleasant, but she'd found her way back from the Sydney Gardens and had lurked on the Common until dawn.

Her thin scarf hadn't been sufficient to keep out the cold and rising damp, and she longed for a long, hot bath.

Mrs. Marshall opened the door. Her jaw dropped. "Jane?"

She smiled sheepishly and lied. "Forgot to put my key in my bag."

"Come in, come in! You must be freezing! I'll put the kettle on."

Jane let her bustle ahead, closing the door behind her with a satisfying snap. She'd been worried Terrance might come upon her on the B&B doorstep before Mrs. Marshall answered the door, but he never was an early riser.

She gazed around the narrow hallway and stepped into the breakfast salon. Something wasn't quite right, and she couldn't put her finger on it.

Dazed, she allowed her fingertips to trail over the backs of chairs, moving slowly to her table. She frowned as Mrs. Marshall reappeared with a tea tray. "You've painted."

Mrs. Marshall's head tilted to one side. "No, dear." She handed Jane a cup. "Drink that, and you will feel better."

Jane accepted the cup and drank from it, wandering about the room. Something felt different, she knew it. Had she changed the future and saved Ramsay and Lydia anyway?

Not that the wretched girl deserved saving, she mentally added with a jealous pang.

She looked at the wall she saw every morning at breakfast time. A still life of a basket of flowers hung there.

She frowned. Where was Lydia's portrait?

She scanned all the walls in the small room. It took all her self-control not to leap up and examine every wall in the house. Where had the tiny painting gone?

What had they done last night that had changed their future? That had removed Lydia from Ramsay's walls? Had he destroyed the picture in anger? Were they both safe?

She couldn't wait to get upstairs to her B&B history binder. Struggling to keep her panic from rising, she took a restoring sip of tea before asking casually, "I'm sure you must've told me, Mrs. Marshall, but what happened to the previous owner of the B&B, the one it's named after?"

Her hostess stared. "Did you have a knock on the head, dear? How could you forget a story like that?"

Jane wished she had. "I've heard so many histories since I've come to Bath, I've got them all muddled, I'm sure. Tell me what happened, please."

"Mr. Chadwick was an up and coming magistrate. His dad was a wealthy merchant and his mum a gentlewoman. He was murdered in 1812 after breaking off his engagement."

She swallowed hard twice. She hadn't saved him. She'd only made it worse. "Murdered?" Her voice crumbled. Ramsay killed? Why?

"Aye, and they never found out who did it either. He's buried in the Abbey. Have you seen his gravestone yet?"

"No," she whispered. She gulped down the remainder of her tea and poured another cup. She needed something stronger, much stronger, but this would have to do.

"What happened to Lydia?" She tried to keep calm. She couldn't go to pieces over a man almost two hundred years dead.

"His fiancée? Oh, she married an even wealthier older man and spent the rest of her life living as she pleased after her husband expired, of pleasure it's said. A real character, that one. She owned this house for a while too."

Numb, Jane finished her tea. Mrs. Marshall retreated to

the kitchen. In moments, the warming scent of bacon entered the breakfast room. Jane's stomach turned at the thought of eating. She ascended the stairs to change out of her Regency gown.

Ramsay had been killed, murdered. The words repeated in her brain until she thought she'd go mad. What had ever made her think she'd be of any use to him? She'd ruined her own life, haunted by a violent stalker, and now she'd destroyed Ramsay's. She'd destroyed all his hopes and had murdered him into the bargain.

She showered, letting the tepid water cascade over her, not wanting to think, not wanting to feel. Back in jeans and a long-sleeved white blouse, she left the B&B after a quick breakfast.

She had to see for herself. She had to see Ramsay's—it hurt just to think it—his gravestone. She wouldn't cry until then—maybe Mrs. Marshall got the years wrong, and it was a few years from now—from then—and . . .

Her throat felt dry, compressed, making it difficult to swallow. Somehow, she made it down Gay Street in her daze and across to the Abbey.

She entered the Abbey via the side door, the gigantic main doors permanently locked. She stood in the crowded vestibule, sealed off from the rest of the church by almost black wood carved into gothic windows. Chafing at the delay, she shuffled forward as tourists paid their two pound fifty to enter the church.

At last she was properly inside. She stopped at the head of the center aisle, staring up at the gorgeous stained glass windows, the rich hues taking her breath away.

But only for a moment.

The abbey's walls were blanketed with marble memorial tablets of all shapes and sizes until there was hardly any wall space left. How would she ever find him?

At once, she discounted the ornate gilt and black marble

tomb toward the front left of the Abbey. It was far too grandiose, not to mention too expensive, for her Ramsay.

Tears of frustration and hopelessness threatened to blank out the interior of the Abbey altogether. She gazed up at the intricate fanned ceiling, wishing her tears would disappear.

A sonorous voice droned in discussion above the rubbered squeaks of tourists' feet on the slate floors, and the sharp tap of a walking cane punctuated the echoing drone of voices in the great space.

She spotted an elderly man wearing Marian blue academic robes and linked him with the sonorous voice. He had to be one of the volunteer guides.

She approached, her tension reaching a finely strung pitch. What would she do if she couldn't find him? She knew he was dead, so what difference would it make? But her logical mind had no say in the convulsions of her heart. She had to see. She had to know.

Jane almost bolted from the church. It would be easier not to see the place marking his tomb. She shuddered. She could be walking over him at this very moment.

The elderly man turned to her, a welcoming smile on his face. A round badge on his robes, a silver sword crossed with a gold bar, flowed out of sight. "May I help you, miss?"

She flashed him a brief, shaky smile. Still young enough to be called 'miss'—that felt nice. "I'm looking for a particular memorial. Ramsay Chadwick?"

"Ah!" The elderly man's eyes lit up. "The murdered magistrate. My great-great-grandfather worked for him as a stable boy. This way, please. Are you staying at the bed and breakfast?"

"Yes." His words had faded after "murdered," but she managed to regain the thread of his chatter just in time. She dutifully followed him down the side aisle, stepping around the tourists who craned to decipher the Latin texts.

"Here it is." Her guide stopped halfway down the Abbey. He pointed to a white marble tablet. A simple oval, probably all Ramsay could afford and yet still hideously expensive, had aged to a mottled beige, the inscription fading. A simple raised rim edged it, the only other ornamentation being a set of scales collapsed at the top.

She stared. *Departed This Life. RAMSAY GOODWIN CHADWICK,* the bold Roman letters were engraved into the stone. *Born 5th October, 1780, Died September 5th, 1812.*

"Tomorrow," she breathed, doing the date conversion in her head.

"Pardon?"

"Only thirty-two," she whispered as a hasty but heart-felt cover-up. *Thirty-two. He'd had his whole life ahead of him. Even alone without Lydia as a wife, wasn't that better than death?*

"Yes indeed. My great-great-grandfather was ten at the time."

She shot him a startled glance, his earlier remarks clicking into place. "Billy?"

"Why yes, that was his name! William. How did you know?"

She cursed her impulsive tongue, returning her attention to the marble stone. The question was impossible to answer. He must think her crazy as it was, but she didn't care. Insanity was nothing beside failure.

"I'll leave you to it." He retreated, leaving her alone.

There was an additional inscription in Latin: *in iustitia veritas.* That had been his downfall. He had to know the truth of everything and everyone, even her. Even if it meant his death, as it clearly had.

She brushed her fingertips over his name. The stone bit cold and she snatched them away, the marble far colder than it should have been at this summery time of year.

"Don't blame me," she whispered, a band of pain burning her ribcage. "I warned you this would happen."

She retreated, feeling a squared pew back bump against her hip. The wooden pew gave a squeak of protest as she sat. She hid her mouth, which worked with suppressed emotion. She stared at it until the tablet blurred from sight.

She couldn't bear to look anymore, gazing at the sun-touched side aisle's ceiling. Golden-hued fans of stone met in heraldic badges and drop points.

The great central space of the Abbey swallowed much of the sound from the murmuring tourists, leaving only echoes.

His memorial stone drew her back again, and she looked at it, wishing it had had the decency to disappear in the interval since she had looked away. The words inscribed had long since stopped making any sense.

Gone.

Her rational mind tried to bank down the rising hysterics. Of course he was dead, gone these last 180 years and more. Nobody lived that long.

It didn't help. He should've lived longer, much longer.

She rubbed at her streaming nose and let the tears come.

*Ramsay!* Her heart cried out to the dead man, the tears spilling over. *Why didn't you heed me? Why weren't you better forearmed? Why did you have to die?*

Tears soaked her cheeks, her sobs dry, soft gasps, for although she mourned him, she didn't want to disturb the tourists, who still gave her a wide berth on seeing her tormented face.

Nobody else would cry over a two-hundred-year-old tombstone.

*Except me. For I loved him and couldn't save him.*

Her last thought almost stopped her breath. What a fool she had been.

*I loved him.*

# Chapter Twelve

The newly restored Klais organ sounded out, filling the Abbey's space with more richness and beauty than the faint echoes of humanity. Its sonorous, heavy notes matched Jane's sorrow. At the sheer drama of it, she laughed, her laughter more of a choking cough through her tears. The organ practice couldn't have been better timed, coming when she was so lost in grief and regret.

She wiped her face with her white linen handkerchief, blowing her nose. She still had one night, one night in which to save him.

Tonight. She'd warn Ramsay of the change—murdered now, instead of disappearing—and hopefully prevent disaster.

*I've changed history once; I can do it again.*

She visited the historian Mr. Jenkins again, and he gave her the coroner's report. His body had been found in the river Avon, but he'd been dead before he'd hit the water. The murderer, Jenkins told her cheerfully, had never been found.

Hours later, the sun had set. She'd been waiting in her room, dressed in her simplest Regency gown, for the past hour. She sat on the bed, the faint beeping of the ghost hunter equipment coming from its concealed places.

She'd spent the day with the ghost hunters, letting them run psychometric tests to measure her natural psychic ability and finding she had none.

"You must be a conduit," the older ghost hunter had said. "Like a magnifying glass."

"Amazing," she had muttered, escaping their offices and going back to the B&B. She felt like an empty conduit, all cried out.

The hours passed. Her hands twisted in her lap, her feet twitched with impatience. She wanted to pace, but would she be able to reach him if he entered while she wasn't on the bed? The only time their connection had failed was when she'd stood up to touch him. *Where was he?*

He had to come tonight; he had to!

She retreated into the center of the bed, propping herself up against the headboard. Pulling the history of the B&B from the bedside table, she reread it, finding some of the details changed since she'd read it after Ramsay's first appearance. It mentioned Ramsay's tragic, unsolved murder and Lydia taking ownership soon after.

Anything written after Ramsay's death failed to hold her interest and the words blurred before her heavy eyes.

Why didn't he come?


Jane woke with a start. Morning light trailed through the window. Her room remained empty, unchanged.

He hadn't come.

Her balled fists rubbed at her eyes. Of course he hadn't. He'd told her as much at the Gardens. He didn't want her help anymore, didn't want to see her again. Clearly, he meant to stick to that.

She got the hint, but refused to take it.

Not that he'd given her any choice in the matter.

She changed into her twenty-first century gear and descended to breakfast. The ghost hunters were already there, poring over fresh readouts. The younger one glared at her.

"He didn't show," she said, passing their table.

The young ghost hunter shook the printouts at her. "We can see that."

She shrugged and turned her attention to breakfast.

What could she do now? Ramsay was beyond her reach and would be dead within 24 hours based on the date on his memorial stone.

She didn't want to go out, although she supposed she should see something more of the city. It had been three days since Terrance had attacked her and she hadn't seen him since. He was either being cleverer about concealing himself, or he'd given up and gone. Jane hoped it was the latter, for she hadn't felt the eerie presence of anyone trailing her in her brief forays to the bottom of town.

Emboldened, she left the B&B after breakfast. This time she walked east through the Circus to the Assembly Rooms. A morning of fashion would turn her mind from Ramsay's absence.

In the shadowy basement of the Assembly Rooms where the costumes were displayed, a Regency gown stopped her in her tracks. It looked to be in pristine condition, never worn. She punched in the number of the audio guide. "This gown belonged to Mrs. Lydia Sandeford. It was found, still in its wrappings from the seamstress, in a trunk in the attic of her Royal Crescent townhouse . . ."

Staring at it, Jane knew with a certainty Lydia had never seen this gown. Ramsay had had it made for her, for Jane. She'd never worn it, having supplied her own wardrobe. How foolish of her not to have accepted one of his gowns. Why it would've been authentic!

She stepped back from the glass, choking down her hysteria.

It would have been something to remember him by, something more than the memories she now had.

Tonight was her last chance to warn him, assuming the worst hadn't happened to him already. What if he didn't show up? Was there anything she could do to compel him to appear? Maybe a psychic . . . But if she reached an already dead Ramsay, he couldn't tell his alive self, could he? He'd just be ticked off that she'd informed him after the fact.

And the truth was, she still didn't know how he died. He'd been murdered, but the murderer had never been captured. He had not been drowned; that was her only clue.

She had failed him, failed whoever or whatever had decided to make her a "conduit." If he didn't appear in her room tonight, he'd be lost to her for good.

She drifted out of the Costume Museum, ascending to the Assembly Rooms above, so empty. Here, she'd danced with him and, on leaving, had lectured him on behaving more like a gentleman toward Lydia. Lectures that had come to naught.


Ramsay ended his court session early, but instead of returning home, he headed downhill for the Abbey. The cheery faces of the shoppers grated on him as he ducked down the side of the Bridge and along the Parades. A few promenaded here, not many; it was no longer fashionable, and it was early in the season.

The sky seemed impossibly blue, a pleasant change from the series of gray and miserable days, but he had already seen clouds hovering on the hillside above the city.

He stepped into the Abbey via one of the side entrances and located the rector in his office off one of the side chapels. He paused in the doorway, feeling foolish.

The rector looked up. He was a man of middle age, round-faced and in boisterous health. "Mr. Chadwick, such a plea-sure to see you and not on a Sunday."

Ramsay nodded. "I was not aware the Abbey was banned to the Corporation on other days."

"Of course not. Come and sit down." The rector asked, "What can I do for you? I heard that your nuptials are off."

"Yes." It actually felt good to say that. "I have come to en-quire about a memorial tablet."

"A—" The rector peered over his round eyeglasses. "I would rather counsel you, my son, in giving yourself a chance to overcome this upset and to advise you that suicides will not be interred within the walls."

"I understand that," Ramsay snapped. "But with no par-ents, no siblings, and now no wife or hope of children to fol-low me, I would like to take care of matters now. I assure you, I have no intention of dying just yet."

Never mind that his need to keep everything neat had dri-ven him here. What if he couldn't fend off this disappear-ance? He had to leave something for her.

For Jane.

"You are handsome and wealthy, Mr. Chadwick, there will be another girl suitable to be your bride."

No, there would not be, but he was not about to argue with the man over it.

He rose. "If you do not see the need, then I will not purchase one." He saw the rector's eyes dim with the realization of a missed opportunity. "I had thought to pay for something small now and perhaps add to it every five or ten years or so."

If he lived, he silently amended.

"Sit down, Mr. Chadwick. Never let it be said that I would refuse one of my parishioner's dearest wishes." He pulled out a large black book and opened it. "Now, what would you like on it?"

It didn't matter. "The usual, I expect."

"Any particular phrase or verse?"

He shifted in his chair. "It does not seem right to create one's own tombstone."

"Memorial tablet," the rector corrected. "Come, we must have something more than your name and dates."

Ramsay thought, rubbing his lower lip.

"How about *in iustitia veritas?* You can change it at any time. Perhaps when you've thought more."

"That will be fine." He nodded, filled with an urge to escape. What was he doing, giving into his presumed destiny. Nothing was fixed until it had happened. He had time yet.

He stood. "Thank you again for seeing to this." He bowed and excused himself. He returned to the inn, catching his clerk in time to obtain his register.

In his study, Ramsay pored over the small book, squinting at the crabbed hand by the study's candlelight. Jane had thought that their deaths had had something to do with an open case before him, but he couldn't find a connection.

Correction, he *wouldn't* make the connection. It had to be tied up in the forged bank notes. And Lydia. He feared she was more involved than he was willing to admit. Wearily, he rubbed at his hair. He needed more facts.

But not from Jane. He'd been heartless, but she inspired confusion in his mind and his heart. Had she tried to stop him from seeing Lydia coupling with Darby to protect him or to ensure the wedding went ahead?

He'd shaken off her attempts at comforting afterward. He didn't want that. That one moment had destroyed his life. Until then he'd been able to salvage some small hope that she—that Lydia—would come in time to love him.

Her betrayal had shattered that forever.

And how did his Jane figure in all of this? He'd stayed away for a night, trying to sort this out on his own, but ultimately, he'd gotten no further than one assumption after another. There was nothing he hated more than assumptions. He wanted simple, easy facts, but none were forthcoming.

His butler appeared in the doorway. "Mrs. Devereaux is here to see you."

Ramsay blinked. "I am not at home. I have nothing more to say to her."

Mrs. Devereaux forced her bulk past the butler. "Yes, you do. What have you done with my daughter?"

He closed the register but didn't bother to rise; he ignored the tiny shaft of panic buried deep. Were Jane's premonitions coming to pass? "I have no idea, madam," he said calmly. "I have not seen her since yesternight."

"And Miss Leighton?" The woman vibrated with some mysterious tension.

What did Jane have to do with anything? "She has gone also."

She jabbed the point of her umbrella in his direction. "Two unmarried women gone! Disappeared! You are a murderer!"

*So the time has come.*

He stood. "Mrs. Devereaux, you are not yourself." He nodded to the butler who grabbed her arms, looking worried at so handling a gentlewoman. "If you will excuse me, I will return in one moment."

He strode from the study, Mrs. Devereaux's hysterical shrieks about bringing the full force of the law down on him rising up the stairwell behind him.

He had no doubt that Mrs. Devereaux was correct in her fears. Lydia was dead, or about to become so. And he would be next. Jane had never revealed the exact date, but her recent agitation suggested it was soon.

He'd not abandon Lydia to her fate. No matter her betrayal. He simply could not.

He'd never wanted to see Jane again, but as much as he hated to admit it, he needed her. If her presence gave him the edge in defeating their fatal destinies, then by God, he would use that advantage.

He swung open the door to his bedchamber and rocketed to a halt. Two ghostly forms writhed on his bed.

His skin went cold, his forehead clammy. *She brought a lover here? Here?*

He squeezed shut his eyes, blocking the vision of their ferocious coupling. Did she do this to spite him? If so, then good riddance! He'd find the missing Lydia himself.

He opened his eyes, his gaze filling with the impassioned scene before him. Her lover lay atop her between her parted legs, which kicked with ecstasy. His hand clamped over her mouth, and her eyes were wide with . . . terror?

No, that wasn't right.

Nobody treated a woman like that. Especially not his Jane.

He closed the distance between himself and the bed and hauled her lover off. The man rolled onto his bed, warm human flesh, ready to spring at him.

Ramsay didn't plan on giving him that chance.

He grabbed the man by his heavy jacket and shoved him against the wall. He released him only to pound the man's face with his fists.

His opponent's fists whirled, but he'd not Ramsay's gentlemanly education.

Ramsay grinned, feeling the satisfying smack of skin against skin, knuckle grinding against bone. It hurt like the very devil, but he welcomed the pain. He hadn't yet called out Darby for the insult to his honor, but at least he could make this fellow pay for his assault on his Jane.

The man stopped resisting, sliding nervelessly down the paneled wall. Ramsay stopped when he found he had to stoop in order to hit him with sufficient force.

Shaking, he stepped back, taking deep, steadying breaths.

He glanced down at his split and bloodied knuckles and flexed his fists. His anger subsided.

He'd lost control. Again.

He glanced at the bed. A ghostly Jane clung to one of the bedposts, curled around with silent sobs.

He'd become a monster before her again. After he had promised not to. He winced, starting to turn from her too. She was his biggest mistake and his undoing.

She reached for him, her arm trembling.

Without volition, he touched her fingertips.

Her sobs became audible, heartbroken.

He ended their fragile connection.

"Are—are you all right?" she managed through the sobs.

"Yes," he ground out, agonized that he'd brought her forth again to witness his humiliation.

"Thank God you're alive." She leapt from her coiled position by the bedpost and flung her arms around him.

Confused by her curious exclamation, he couldn't prevent her embrace.

Her cheek pressed against his buttoned waistcoat. "Thank you. I—I don't know what I would've done if—if you hadn't come . . ." His arms came up around her and he patted her back awkwardly. Her words disintegrated into incoherent sobs.

His embrace convulsed tightly. She'd been in danger, horrible danger, and he'd saved her from a fate worse than death.

When her sobs had quieted, he pried her away, gazing down. "Are you unhurt?" he asked, seeing a bruise rising on her cheekbone. He gritted his teeth, wanting to pummel the oaf again. Her shirt had been torn apart.

She pulled the shirt ends over the odd lacy bandeau around her breasts and brushed her sore cheek. "It could be worse."

She sank onto the bed, staring at the unconscious form of her attacker.

"Who is he?" He tried to gentle his voice, but the anger still swelled within him.

"Terrance. The man who wouldn't let go of me. His wife threw him out." She looked up. "He was hiding here in my room—your room," she amended, her voice growing stronger. "I didn't even get a chance to scream." Her palm covered a repressed sob.

He reached out, but she waved him off.

"No, no. I'll be fine. What are we going to do with him?"

Unaccountably hurt by her rejection, he used one of his outstretched arms to tug on the bell pull. "Trenby and I will take care of him. Tie him up and make him comfortable until the dawn takes him back." He frowned. "How will you explain him being in your room?"

"I'll stick to the truth as much as I can. He attacked me, he was overpowered, and I tied him up before calling the police." She crossed her legs. Her legs weren't bare at all but encased in some sort of heavy blue cotton.

"Police?" He hadn't quite managed to lift his gaze from her lower limbs. They were charming, slender, and—

"You'll have them in a few years. More organized than the Bow Street Runners." She paused. "Ramsay, you look a bit funny. Are you sure you're all right?"

He dragged his gaze upward, examining the bed canopy. He shouldn't leer at her, not after such a shock. He cleared his throat. "Fine, I'm fine." He'd forgotten the reason he'd come up there in the first place. "You can't wear that"—he pointed in the direction of her too revealing clothing—"downstairs."

"They're called jeans. Very comfortable."

"I thought those were invisible building blocks?" They looked anything but invisible to him. Not that they left much to the imagination as to the shape and form of her legs.

A hint of a smile crossed her face. "Do I have to go down?"

"Yes. Mrs. Devereaux thinks I've murdered her daughter—and you."

"Oh dear." Her voice wobbled, close to the point of hysteria. He hoped she'd resist. He needed his sensible Jane now.

"I have a gown for you." He flushed. In his rage, he'd ordered it put away. "It's up in the attic somewhere."

His valet, Trenby, appeared, his eyes widening in surprise at the sight of the unconventionally dressed Jane.

Ramsay couldn't blame him. He had difficulty not looking at the swell of her breasts or her slim legs. "Trenby, fetch some rope to bind this rascal, and have those gowns brought down from the attic for Miss Leighton."

"Yes, sir." Trenby bowed himself out, his gaze discreetly lowered.

Ramsay knelt to check Terrance's pulse and found it steady. "He's going to survive." He straightened. "I'm sorry if I shocked you when I—" He gestured at the villain.

"Shocked me? It's the best thing that's ever happened!" She leapt to her feet but shuddered to a halt. "I was suffocating when I saw you. I didn't think I—I would . . ."

"Would what? See me alive again?"

She nodded, her gaze sharp. "How did you know?"

"Because Lydia's gone. It seems she's taken my fate and—"

Jane vigorously shook her head and grabbed at his sleeve. "No, she lives. She lives! We did change history, Ramsay. It's just that you—"

"Die." He finished for her. What else had he left to lose but his life?

He saw her swallow hard.

"Then we shall just have to change history again, won't we?" He wished it would be true. Yet she cheered at his confident words, standing aside to allow him and Trenby to drag Terrance across the floor and tie him to the bedpost.

A maid entered, bearing an armful of dresses wrapped in

natural linen. She placed them on the bed and the odor of cedar and camphor wafted to Jane's nostrils. Jane quirked a smile. Mrs. Devereaux should be able to smell her coming.

He kissed Jane's hand. "Come downstairs when you are ready. My poor butler probably has been forced to tie up Mrs. Devereaux as well."

She echoed his strained smile and he left her with the maid, heading downstairs to calm Mrs. Devereaux and his own thoughts. Her daughter would still be alive at the end of this night after all.

He reviewed the conflagration of emotions the last few minutes had wrought. Why had he felt so betrayed by Jane taking a lover? They had kissed but once, and she could never be his. They moved in two different worlds, only occasionally connecting. She should be free to live as she chose.

That is how it had been with her and always would be. He accepted that, for he had no choice. He thought of her glimmering eyes bravely meeting his while he consoled her in his arms. How he wished it could be otherwise.

Mrs. Devereaux paced in an agitated fashion behind the long sofa in his drawing room. "I heard banging and thumping up there! What were you doing?"

Ramsay concealed his battered knuckles behind his back. "Nothing to do with your daughter, I assure you. I am quite certain she is safe, Mrs. Devereaux. Did you check with her paramour as to her location?"

"He knew nothing!"

His eyebrow twitched. "And I would because . . . ?"

"She used you most dreadfully, Mr. Chadwick. You left in a most foul temper. Any mother would fear for her daughter's life in those circumstances."

"May I remind you, Mrs. Devereaux, that I am a gentleman? No matter what Lydia has done, I would not harm one hair on her head." He heard footsteps thudding down the

stairs and along the hallway. He smiled at the pause that followed. No doubt his Jane did some last minute tidying from
her helter-skelter rush.

Instead, his butler entered bearing a letter on a silver salver,
Jane trailing behind. "Lydia's sent a note," she announced before the butler delivered it. *"He* wouldn't let me read it." She
shot the butler a daggered look.

Ramsay retrieved the letter, breaking the plain wax seal. "It
is best if we read it together."

Jane leaned on his arm, trying to peer at the words. "You
should employ Lydia for your clerk; she has perfect handwriting."

Ignoring the astonished Mrs. Devereaux and daring to enjoy
Jane's closeness, he read the brief contents and folded the paper.
"Mrs. Devereaux, it seems your mother's intuition is somewhat
correct. Lydia has got herself into some difficulty."

His butler hovered. "Shall I call out the watch?"

"No need," he replied, flinching at Jane's muffled cry of
fear. He didn't want to cause her pain, but the watchmen of
Bath would be about as much use as—well, a match in a
paper warehouse. "I need a small bag. Meet me in my study."

The butler bowed and let himself out.

He broke the connection between himself and Jane, crossing
to Mrs. Devereaux, handing her the note, and guiding her to sit.
"She's being held for ransom. I will get her back for you."

"Ransom?" Mrs. Devereaux's fan fluttered furiously. She
read the note. "We have not the funds . . ."

"That is why she has applied to me for help. I will go—"

*"We* will go," Jane interrupted, glaring at him with such a
determined look, he hadn't the heart to refuse her. It would be
dangerous, but perhaps, just perhaps, Jane would be his good
luck charm. She had managed to save Lydia at least.

"Oh, Mr. Chadwick, how can I ever thank you!" Mrs.

Devereaux blubbered. "Forgive me for all my harsh words earlier. If I had only known my girl—"

He waved her to silence. "If we are not back—"

"Don't say it," Jane murmured, touching his arm again.

He patted her hand in reassurance. "I have some money in a safe in my study. We must leave at once. Who knows how long this tyrant will keep Lydia unharmed." He gazed down at Mrs. Devereaux. "Will you stay here or wait at home?"

"At home. I will prepare my poor baby a posset to calm her nerves for she will surely need it."

Mrs. Devereaux looked like she could use one of her potions too. "Good woman," he approved, relieved. He didn't want to bring Lydia back here. He could trust Jane to take care of matters for him if he didn't make it.

Taking Jane's hand in his, he left the drawing room for the study. Her hand felt small within his, but she held on tight. She said nothing to him, disengaging when they reached the safe.

He felt her gaze upon him as he filled the small bag with bank notes and coins. He rose and smiled at her, pleased when she essayed a small smile in return.

She did not speak, did not try and dissuade him from his course, and he silently thanked her for it.

If these were his last hours on earth, at least he got to spend them in her company. He'd never tell her these thoughts, knowing that they would only hurt her.

"Shall we go?"


The carriage rattled over the Pulteney Bridge and through the hamlet of Bathwick. "But why at your country house?" Jane asked, hanging onto a strap of leather for dear life as they were jolted about the speeding carriage's interior.

"No doubt because my driver knows the way sufficiently well not to take a wrong turn in getting there."

Jane muffled a snort. He had no idea then. She wished she could see him, but it was too dark. The interior carriage lights had been doused so hot wax wouldn't spatter on them on rounding a curve. He sounded so calm and collected, yet she'd sensed the high tension in him while they prepared to leave.

She hadn't asked questions then, too afraid that her presence would only seal Ramsay's death. "Who has her, do you think?"

"We shall find out soon enough, Jane," came his unruffled response. "I suspect it has something to do with the forged notes, but we won't know until we get there."

"How can you be so calm?" She grimaced at the fear in her voice, but who was she kidding? She was scared. Terrified. Unless she did something, Ramsay would die tonight—and her track record to date didn't exactly inspire confidence.

"Come here," his soft and gentle voice cajoled. She extended her hand and found him reaching for her in the dark. Her fingers closed around his hand and he reversed the grip, pulling her toward him.

She surrendered her safety to his arms. Face pressed against his coat jacket, she inhaled deeply. She wanted to remember everything about him, even down to the scent of him, of soap and sandalwood.

His lips pressed against her forehead. "If I am to die, then I plan on going out with calm dignity, not railing against God and the world for not allowing me something that I want." He kissed her hair.

A tear slipped from between her eyelids, absorbed by his coat's heavy felt. "I think that after you, Ramsay Chadwick, I'm going to give up men."

His chest shook with sudden, suppressed laughter. "You?"

She bristled at that, pulling away from him. "Yes, me. It's not so impossible." He'd reminded her of her failings, the disastrous relationships that never worked. "After all, they never work. Not even this one."

She could've bitten off her tongue. What was she thinking, to share that her feelings for him were more than friendship? Well, he *had* kissed her.

"Indeed, Miss Leighton." His cold response made her shiver. "I suppose I should be flattered and yet it is not exactly illustrious company I keep, is it, with your past beaus."

"Ouch." She slid further from him. She wouldn't give him satisfaction by telling him how unlike the others he was. "You haven't joined that crew yet, Ramsay Chadwick. You're better off without me. Not that I think that it's possible for me to make your life even more of a misery than I already have."

There. She'd said it.

"Hmm."

She wished she could unsay the self-pitying words, the words that locked Ramsay out of her life with more finality than the coming dawn. But they had been said, and any connection they had was sundered.


Jane stared up at the shadowy walls of Ramsay's country house. Far to the east, she spied the soft glow of Bath. There were farmer's houses here and there out on the black, rolling hills, but their lights were extinguished at this late hour. The night was always darkest before the dawn, the saying went, and dawn was a few hours away.

"Stay here," Ramsay ordered their driver.

Uneasy, Jane clutched his arm, accepting one of the carriage lanterns from him. "Are you sure that's wise?"

"I don't want to spook whoever has Lydia. Besides, I am not unarmed." He patted his pocket and pointed to a window on the far right. "Look there." A faint reddish glow came from one of the windows in the night-hidden facade. "Someone's lit a fire. Come on."

They walked to the front door, the gravel crunching loudly

with each step. If perchance whoever awaited them hadn't heard the carriage and horses already, the gravel screeched out further warnings. *We're coming. Get ready.*

Ramsay pushed on the door and it opened easily. Her lamp's light glimmered off the walls, picking up gilt on picture frames and the glint of mirrors. "I had this place almost ready for her," he muttered, leading her to the right, toward the lit fireplace.

The lamp revealed the truth of his words. Large dustcloths lay over furniture. Some had been turned back, revealing polished wood: a chair, a turned table leg.

She tried not to think about Ramsay's peaceful, bucolic life should he live tonight, unlikely though that might be. She gave herself a shake. She had to stop thinking of him gone. The last thing he needed was a blubbering female on his hands.

In the next room, a lamp flared into life. Ramsay stopped short, pushing Jane behind him. Blinking the light from her eyes, she peered around him into the room.

Lydia sat on a chair, her mouth bound and her long, blond hair falling in disarray about her shoulders. Her hands were tied behind her back.

"You!" Ramsay snapped at the room's other occupant, his right hand delving into his pocket.

"Not so fast, old man." Smiling, Darby directed his pistol at Lydia. "You don't want her to get hurt."

Jane drew forward to Ramsay's side, refusing to hide. She'd see this to the bitter end.

"Ah, and you brought your pretty little mistress along too! I may take my pleasure from her as well before this night is done."

Ramsay advanced and was checked by the jerk of the pistol barrel in his direction before Darby pointed back at Lydia.

"Really, I mean it. I will kill her, and you, and your mistress before this night is done. Do you have the money?"

Prying Jane's hand free from his arm, he patted his left pocket. "It is here. I do not understand. What need do you have of money?"

"I'm stone cold stony broke." Darby's broad grin seemed at odds with this turn of events.

"I could have loaned you funds. You didn't have to go to— to these lengths." He gestured at the wild-eyed Lydia.

"Oh, but I did. Borrowing means having to pay you back, and I had no intention of ever doing that. Even making forged notes didn't make ends meet. I gave them to her, did you guess?"

From Ramsay's composed features, Jane realized he'd guessed that much. "I would not have asked for repayment until you were able . . ."

"Able?" Darby barked a brief laugh. "That would require making sound investments, going into *business*." His voice filled with disdain on the word. "And all the time taking your damned superior attitude. Yes, your papa made your money, but you made more out of it." His lip curled. "I couldn't stand your self-righteous pity, you damnable prig." He stuck out his hand. "Now give me the blunt."

Slowly, Ramsay withdrew the heavy leather pouch from his pocket. "Release Lydia."

"Naturally, old boy." Chuckling, Darby tugged at the gag's knot behind Lydia's head. "Tell him, Lyds."

Jane's stomach roiled uneasily. She'd never been in a hostage situation before, but she'd seen plenty of them on TV. The villain had just revealed his motive. Now he and the hero had to battle for the right to the imperiled damsel. Meanwhile, an oncoming train raced down the tracks . . .

This wasn't the movies or even the Saturday morning cartoons. The damsel in distress never had a say.

"Tell me what?" Ramsay's sharp-edged voice cut across the silence.

Lydia smiled. "With your money and my dowry, we'll have enough for a passage to America."

But she didn't go, Jane's foreknowledge kicked in. She frowned. Lydia had stayed in Bath. What had happened to make her stay?

"We're starting over fresh, free of all debts." Lydia reached up to take Darby's hand in hers. With a sharp intake of breath, Jane realized Lydia's hands had never been tied.

"I have her dowry already." Jane didn't think Darby's grin could get any more wolfish. "Truth be told, I do not need her anymore." He snatched his hand free of hers and, with a stiff arm, shoved her shoulder.

Lydia sprawled onto the parquet floor, sliding a few feet before coming to a stop, the skirts of her white gown trailing behind her. She flipped onto her back, wailing her betrayal.

Ramsay bent toward her, his hand outstretched to help up his fallen ex-fiancée.

"In fact," Darby drawled, raising his pistol, "I don't need any of you alive. I'll be long gone by the time they find your bodies in the river." He took aim.

"No!" Jane propelled herself forward, flying in front of Ramsay.

The impact ripped through her, stealing her breath. She landed in an ungainly lump on the floor, sliding a small way before coming to a stop.

Whoever had waxed Ramsay's floors had done an excellent job.

She hiccuped, a flare of pain jolting her ribs. Why couldn't she breathe?

A second shot rang out. She tried to scream. Had Darby a second pistol? Did her Ramsay lie dying nearby? No sound came from between her lips.

That's right. She couldn't breathe.

She gasped. *No. That . . . that was a breath, wasn't it? Ok, lungs, now you just have to inflate again . . .*

Someone lifted her head. She tried focusing on the blurred face above hers. Why couldn't she see? Ah, her cheeks were wet. It must really hurt.

"Jane! Jane! Dear sweet God! Jane!"

*Ramsay.* She smiled inwardly. Whether or not her mouth obeyed her command, she didn't know, didn't care. Ramsay lived. She had saved him.

A weight pressed down near her shoulder, making the hurt flare into fresh life. She let out a pained whimper. She didn't have the strength for more than that. Her senses screamed with the wrongness of it. At the back of her throat she tasted a metallic tang.

She swallowed hard. She was in Ramsay's arms, bleeding all over him no doubt.

And she was dying.

The blackness swallowed her. His name formed on her lips. "Ramsay . . ."

"Don't speak, don't speak," his soft voice urged. He sounded blurry to her. Had her ears filled with her tears? "Just stay with me, Jane. Promise me, stay with me."

She blinked away the tears to see for just a moment, his face above hers. Ravaged with grief, trails of tears marked his reddened features.

*I really am dying.* Her fingers curled in sudden fear. *Ramsay! You live! Thank God. I'm sorry . . .*

She thought the room lightened for a moment before she felt nothing at all.

# Chapter Thirteen

Blinding white. Jane's eyelids fluttered and the fluorescent lights calmed down into something only slightly less eye-watering. She felt pleasantly numb.

And then she remembered.

Ramsay. Darby's pistol firing. Ramsay.

Her hand felt heavy, too heavy to lift. She tried anyway, bringing it up to her face, blinking to focus. A clear plastic tube ran along the back of her hand.

Plastic? She tried to process the thought. She'd made it home?

With infinite patience, she turned her head to one side. A drip dangled from a metal rack.

She blinked. She lived.

When her head returned to its original position to gaze at the ceiling, she found a new face in the periphery of her vision.

He wore a uniform. Dark blue. A policeman. She felt quite clever for working that out.

"Miss Jane Leighton?"

"Yes?" She coughed, her mouth dry.

"Can you remember what happened?"

Of course she could remember what happened. But no way

in hell would the constable ever get to hear it. "Not really," she hedged.

"Could you explain why a Mr. Terrance Rayce was found tied up in your room at the Chadwick B&B?"

So it was still a bed and breakfast then? Had she failed to change the past after all? And Ramsay?

"Miss Leighton?" the constable prodded.

Only Ramsay called her that. She closed her eyes, rested for a moment, and then opened them again. Everything seemed to be an effort. *Oh yes, the question.* "He broke into my room and attacked me when I came back from dinner." Exactly what she told Ramsay she'd say. The tears welled in her eyes. What had happened to him?

"And then?"

She didn't know what happened next. She had to talk to that historian, Mr. Jenkins. Oh, he meant about Terrance. "I won and tied him up. Then I went out—"

"You didn't call the police?"

She somehow managed an apologetic smile. Her lips cracked. She winced. "Sorry. I thought I'd teach him a lesson and call the police in the morning. It was very late, and I didn't really want to disturb Mrs. Marshall's other guests."

"How did you overpower him?"

She tried to shrug. Pain lanced through her left shoulder. She swore profusely, blinking away the tears. "How did I get here?"

"You were found bleeding in the middle of the road. A lorry almost ran you over." He repeated his earlier question.

She winced. "Ouch. I'm sorry, I don't remember what happened. Am I going to be okay?"

"I'll leave that to the doctor, but considering she's allowing you visitors, I'd say yes." He flipped open a fresh page in his notebook. "You're a visitor to Bath, correct?" She nodded. "Is—" he hesitated. "Is there some sort of gang warfare going on between the reenactment groups?"

She just stared at him.

"You were shot with a . . . ahh, lead bullet from a nineteenth century firearm. You were wearing a Regency gown and well . . ."

Jane broke into hysterical laughter and continued despite the shocking pain until the red-faced police officer called in a nurse. The needle mercifully dulled her emotions and allowed sleep to reclaim her.


Jane sent Mr. Jenkins a note, but it took him a few days to respond. She spent that time in mental agony, wondering what had become of Ramsay. She felt sure that he had survived that evening, but had fate claimed him again soon after? Had he and Lydia married after all? If it wasn't for the pain medication, sleep would've been impossible. The nightmares were bad enough. By the time Mr. Jenkins showed up, she was in a welter of impatience.

"I don't usually do house calls," Mr. Jenkins grumped, taking a seat.

"I guess I'm lucky you take hospital calls then," Jane snapped.

"If you're going to take that tone, young lady." He started to rise.

"It's the pain, I'm sorry," she apologized. She had to know. "I need to know what happened to Ramsay Chadwick."

For some reason, that made Mr. Jenkins sit. "The strange thing is, that's why I came. I know you've been researching this Chadwick fellow, but I couldn't for the life of me figure out why. He lived a relatively long, quiet, and unassuming life."

Jane exhaled slowly, the tension dissipating. He had lived. "He married?"

"No. Remained a bachelor all his life." Mr. Jenkins's eyes narrowed. "Now, there's something you must tell me. When you called and asked what had happened to him after 1812, I did some research on the fellow.

"It was a curious year to pick. Seems that it was the most eventful in that fellow's life. He got engaged, broke off his engagement, got shot at, and implicated a prominent citizen in bank fraud."

"Implicated?" She hadn't really cared what happened to Darby, so long as Ramsay remained safe.

"He fled the country, which surprised the locals because Chadwick had reported that he'd shot him."

"He lived?"

Mr. Jenkins flipped through his notes. "I don't recall following that path." He pinned her with his sudden sharp gaze. "I found something much more interesting in extant correspondence from Mrs. Devereaux—she was a great letter writer—during this period around the ending of her daughter's engagement."

A trickle of fear ran down her spine. "Oh?"

"Seems one of the reasons for breaking the engagement, aside from her daughter's public humiliation in Sydney Gardens, was that Chadwick was reported to have a mistress. A Miss Jane Leighton. Care to explain?"

Her mind blanked. What could she tell him that he would believe?

"I don't know, Miss Jane Leighton. What can you tell me?" She sucked in a breath. "I said that aloud?" He nodded. "It must be the drugs," she muttered.

"Is she some ancestor of yours, a namesake?"

Wonderfully, brilliantly, Mr. Jenkins had given her the answer she needed. "Yes, yes, that's it."

"Having found you—your name, I went ahead and investigated her as I thought you might like to know, but I am guessing you know more about her than I. There is no mention of her anywhere. You have letters or a journal of hers?"

Jane remained silent, not trusting herself to speak.

"If you would be willing to share these, it may shed some light on an interesting little scandal."

"The thing is, Mr. Jenkins"—Jane had settled on her story—"there is little more than tantalizing hints at it. That's one of the reasons I'm here in Bath, to find out more."

"Do you suppose it has anything to do with your shooting?"

Jane frowned. "Not the reenactment theory again."

"On the contrary, the *Bath Chronicle* was quite detailed about the events of that night. Chadwick and his mistress had gone to rescue his ex-fiancée—very kind of your ancestress, I must say—and the heroics concluded with the mistress being shot and fleeing with the fellow who'd shot her, of all people."

"Darby?" Why would Ramsay concoct a story like that? Did he think her dead? But she wasn't. She had to reach him. She flexed her wounded shoulder and hissed in pain.

"That's his name. She was shot in the left shoulder, in fact. His former fiancée testified to everything that had happened and retired to the country for a little while."

"Did she come back?"

"Indeed, and married a wealthy fellow, who died soon after. Expired of pleasure, according to one nastily written report at the time. But then, he was eighty, so it was just as likely to have been from natural causes. But I'm getting off track here. Don't you find it very interesting that both you and your ancestress have the same injury?"

"Mine wasn't fatal," Jane murmured, wishing her heart would stop pounding quite so hard.

"In 1812, it would have been."

"Then I am very lucky."

He observed her for a long time. Jane held his gaze for as long as she could. She looked away. She'd never thought she'd have unearthed such a mess just because she'd wanted to know about Ramsay. She kept her lips firmly together, refusing to speak her thoughts.

Mr. Jenkins was a smart man. At least she had the advantage that he didn't believe in such hocus pocus as ghosts and time travel.

"I see you will not tell me." He rose, stuffing his notes back into a battered brown briefcase. "If you ever change your mind, I'd like to know the whole story. I surmise that Chadwick's ghost might have something to do with it, but what I don't know."

His pronouncement both thrilled and disturbed her. Ramsay continued to haunt the B&B? But why? By Mr. Jenkins's account, he should be happy and at peace.

"I suggest you leave it at coincidence, Mr. Jenkins," she told him, wondering if she'd spoken aloud again. She'd have to stop taking those drugs. "Thank you for coming and telling me his story."

"Just remember, if you ever change your mind . . ." He left her alone.

Jane closed her eyes, coaxing her limbs to relax. Ramsay had survived. It bothered her that he hadn't married, but perhaps Lydia had burned him too deeply. At least she knew she could say goodbye to him once she was better.

She allowed herself to dream of buying the bed and breakfast and being with Ramsay every night—assuming he wanted her. She could sell her jewelry shop, her apartment in London . . .

She pulled the local newspaper to her, opening it to the real estate section. There was an apartment on the Royal Crescent for sale; maybe she could get Ramsay to move houses and—

"1.5 million pounds? For a flat?"

That was it. There was no way she could even afford the down payment on a flat, let alone an entire building. She would have to let him go.

Tears seeped from between her eyelids as she lay back. She'd been foolish enough to fall in love with him. Leaving Ramsay had torn a hole in her heart more efficiently than any nineteenth-century bullet.

*One month later*

Aching all over, Jane got out of the taxicab. She stared up at the Chadwick B&B's facade. She'd come back to say her goodbyes.

Oh, and collect her luggage, sling or no sling. All of them had wheels anyway. The hospital had let her out at last, and she needed to return to London, back to her work and her friends.

She could have had her luggage sent to her flat in London. She wanted to collect it in person, wanted to see how the place had changed now that she had changed the past.

And say goodbye. Even though he might not hear her.

Mrs. Marshall opened the front door and came out, arms open to her. "Oh, my dear! So kind of you to come back and stay after everything that happened!"

She ushered Jane inside. Jane caught a glimpse of a plaque on the wall by the door. "Official Stop for the Ghost Walkers Tour," she read aloud. "You got it!"

Mrs. Marshall's smile thinned. "Yes, although I regret the day I did so." She lowered her voice. "I used to get respectable people staying here. Now there are some very strange New Agey sorts. This isn't Glastonbury, you know." She gestured to Jane to sit. "Tea will be a minute."

Jane made sympathetic noises when Mrs. Marshall returned. "Is my old room still available?"

The teapot clattered against Jane's teacup, slopping hot brown liquid into the saucer. "There? Why on earth would you want to stay there?"

Jane frowned. She had to see the room one last time. "But I stayed there before."

"But you won't get one wink of sleep!"

*I never did.*

"I never let that room to guests now. I don't know why I even allowed you to stay in it. The ghost is too frightening."

"Frightening?" Jane echoed. "But—"

Why did Ramsay still haunt his old bedchamber? And why had he changed? Was he a real ghost now? She tried to focus on Mrs. Marshall. She needed every clue.

"It was kind of you to be so polite about it before, but you really should've let me know how scary he is. Why, I even tried to spend a night in that room. I should have it exorcised, but according to my lease, I'm not allowed any such procedure."

"Scary?" She found it impossible to comprehend. Oh, she had witnessed him losing his temper, but scary? Ramsay? "What happens?"

Mrs. Marshall's brow wrinkled in confusion. "You know," she told her. "He comes into the room, peers right into your face, and then starts to—starts to—" She turned pale.

"Starts to what?"

"Ranting would be the best word for it. He waves his arms about and yells, even though you can't hear a thing."

Jane's lips quirked. She didn't know why Ramsay was angry each night . . . Unless he looked for her. Was it him or a real ghost trapped by her nineteenth-century murder? But she lived. There was only one way to find out.

"So the only room I have available is up on the top floor in the attics."

"All those stairs?" She made a face. "Please, Mrs. Marshall. I don't fancy lugging my bags all the way up and back down again."

Mrs. Marshall gave her a long look and huffed a resigned

sigh. "All right. You never did complain before, so you must have the stomach for it. The Chadwick room is yours."

Jane grinned, leaping up and giving the woman a one-armed hug. "Thank you!"

"Don't thank me," Mrs. Marshall said, shaking her head. "Here's the key. I'll bring your bags up for you, and don't think of carrying them back down by yourself tomorrow."

"Thank you," Jane said more soberly, already planning ahead. She'd take a nap and then she'd be able to say goodbye to Ramsay in person. She'd find out why he insisted on frightening Mrs. Marshall's guests and then tell him to go live a full life in peace.

Ramsay strode into his bedchamber, glaring at the bed. Another ghostly creature lay there. Why wouldn't they leave him alone? Stupid, vile intruders.

Jane was dead. He'd reconciled himself to that. Her life had ebbed away while he'd held her in his arms, her body vanishing when the dawn came. He'd tried to stop the bleeding. Tried to get her to a surgeon in time.

All for nothing.

He ruffled his hair, already tousled out of its coifed shape by a day of trying to lose himself in work. He wanted his life to return to normal, but it hadn't, and he'd started to wonder if his scattered thoughts would ever recollect.

He hunched his shoulders and prepared to gaze upon the visiting face from the future. He had to look. She had still breathed when the dawn had taken her. There was a slight chance someone had found her and gotten her help in time.

A slim chance, but one he couldn't, wouldn't ignore, even though to look in vain tore him apart each time. The pain of not finding her never diminished, as he thought it might, but drove him to look again and again. It had been a month, now. Maybe he should move, sell the—

His heart stopped. The woman in his bed lay awake, her arm in a sling, watching him with a wary expression.

Jane! But why was she so cautious?

He closed the space between them, settling on the bed and taking her trembling, outstretched hand, thrilling when she transformed into warmth. She lived!

"Jane! My dearest, sweetest Jane!" He gathered her into his arms, careful of her wound, and peppered her face with kisses.

His mouth found hers at last, and her lips seized upon his, kissing him hungrily, eagerly. Their embrace tightened until she moaned into his mouth.

Her muffled cry recalled him to himself. He couldn't kiss her like this, thrilled as he was to see her alive. He pulled back, breathing heavily with restraint. He noticed she was likewise not unaffected. She gingerly touched her shoulder. He controlled a flinch. Had he not taken enough care? Had he hurt her again?

"How bad?" He couldn't not touch her, no matter how much he knew he shouldn't, so he caressed her cheek with the pad of his thumb.

"It's almost better. A fair bit of muscle damage." Her unbound hand covered his. "Apparently, it was touch and go with the amount of blood I lost."

He pulled away, a well of guilt choking off his delight. "I did everything I could."

"I'm going to be fine," she soothed. "I just need some time for the muscles to heal and work them out when they're ready. They've already given me exercises." She showed him a piece of paper crumpled in her lap. "I was reviewing them when you came."

He glanced at the paper, marveling at the detail and clarity of the instructions, and put it aside. He bent his head, pressing his cheek against the smooth warmth of her hand. She was alive. She was real.

She tensed beneath him. "You look like hell."

He released her. "I am fine. I . . . worried about you." Longed for her was the truth of it. "You can still come back." He didn't meet her gaze. His mind raced with the possibilities, the consequences. His heart swelled with hope. Would she want to stay, to keep visiting him?

She grinned at him in her old, carefree way. "And you're scaring the guests. You didn't do that before."

"None of them were you," he murmured. "I cannot be expected to sleep in the same bed as strangers. I had to make them scream to make them go away." He tried to smile, but he knew the dark circles beneath his eyes belied his attempt at levity. "I would that you were in my bed every night."

Her sharp intake of breath sent him wondering. She had kissed him with such voracity. Had he imagined the passion spiraling out of control, or had it all been in his mind, the way he wanted it to be?

"Ramsay . . ." She glanced away from him, at anywhere but him, and he already dreaded what she had to say. His time had almost killed her once. Why would she want to come back again anyway? "I am not worth it, Ramsay. How would it work?"

He didn't want to see that resigned expression on her face. Before she defeated herself, and them, he had to give her a reason to stay. "Jane, we said some things that night that should not have been said."

"They were true."

"Nay, it was our fears speaking, protecting ourselves. Our wounds were too fresh. Ever since I lost you to the dawn, I have wished I could unsay them all."

"But Ramsay—"

He covered her lips with a finger. He had to finish what he

had to say before he lost his nerve and lost her all over again. "I want you, Jane. Not just in my bed but in my life." There, he'd said it. He plunged on. "I've mourned for you every day for the last four weeks, sure you had died."

Her eyes turned silver with tears. "Oh . . ."

He tilted her chin and kissed her again, lightly this time, and felt her respond. Her lips parted beneath his and she leaned into him. She did feel something for him.

She pulled back, taking a shuddering breath. "Ramsay, I came back because I had to say goodbye."

*No! Don't say it!* "Goodbye?" he echoed. The pain of separation twisted in his vitals.

She cradled her bound arm. "You're free now, Ramsay. You will live a long life, but it should be a happy one too. I'm not for you. I'm the wrong girl from the wrong time. It won't work."

"Of course it can work. Jane, if the nights I spend with you are all I can have . . ." He trailed off. He understood. Sharing her nights would make him like all her past lovers, the ones who went back to their wives in the morning. He wouldn't, couldn't do that to her.

"I *can't*." She ducked her head, her lips compressing. Having mastered herself, she met his gaze. "I cannot come back to you every night. I have a business to run, an apartment in London, and I can't afford to stay in this B&B. I can't even afford to buy it."

"How much?"

She exhaled a patient sigh. "I suppose you should know. Two, maybe three million. I can't afford the deposit, let alone the monthly mortgage payments. It's just not possible."

The amount of money boggled his mind. It was enough to buy an entire estate, maybe two. "I understand, Jane." It killed him to say it, but he allowed the mask to rise and conceal his pain. He'd thought about this for a long time.

She stared at him. "You do?"

"You deserve more than I can give you. It is true I am not married or otherwise promised." His lips twisted in a wry grimace. "I am possessed of a good fortune and have an impeccable background when it comes to women." She snorted at that and he couldn't help but grin at her. *Present company excepted,* he thought. "I am not without faults; I have a temper, which is almost always under control.

"The one thing I cannot give you is time, and time is what you need, Jane. I would marry you at midnight, but you need someone to share your nights *and* days with." His throat felt thick with unshed tears. He had her in his arms and he was letting her go.

"As do you," she murmured. "Even if we embarked on this insanity, I couldn't bear it if another woman came into your life. Better to make the break now." A tear slipped down her cheek, followed by another.

"I know." He leaned forward and kissed her, her cheek brushing his shoulder. Aside from his arm pressed against hers, as they both strove to stay balanced, it was all he touched of her. All he dared to, for now.

She loved him. He felt giddy with it. She lived—*she lived!*—and she loved him. He'd known it for a long time, since she'd fought so hard for his happiness. Harder than anyone who had ever cared for him. He hadn't wanted to know, but mourning her had made him realize what he'd been hiding from.

"We are survivors, both of us. Haven't we proven that?" Head bowed, he examined their entwined fingers. "Then we have just one night left to us. Tell me, if you could stay, would you?"

"Of course." Her featherlight touches on his chest, his neck, his cheek, set his heart pounding.

"I—I love you." His cheeks flushed at his blurted declaration.

He shouldn't have said it, shouldn't have tried to bind her to him, but he had to let her know—

Her lips brushed his cheek. "I love you too, Ramsay." She captured his mouth and drew him down to lie beside her on the bed.

He took great pains not to hurt her damaged shoulder. Did she know what she asked with her body?

She twisted beneath him, wrapping her legs around his waist. "If we have just one night," she breathed, "let it be this one." Her fingers tangled in his hair.

He wanted her. He wanted her with every single gene in his body. He loved her even more. It took everything he had to gently disentangle himself from her. He put a little distance between them. "No, Jane."

He died a little at her hurt expression. "Why not?"

"Because it would make it even harder to live without you. To never see you again."

"I'll come back for visits. There's this movie where a couple meets once a year—"

He didn't dare ask what a movie was. "It is too much to ask of you."

She glared at him mulishly. "That is for me to decide. We love each other, Ramsay. Why should we deny it? Any time spent with you . . ." She broke off, looking away.

He hated to reject her again. "It would not be much of a life, being alone for so much of the time."

"Better than being alone forever. History says you never marry, Ramsay."

He knew he never would. With or without her. "Explain your modern banking system to me. There might be a way—"

"I can't take money from you!"

"My dear, independent Jane. You have given me so much. Let me give a little back, and if it means spending more time together . . ." He outlined his plan. He would leave her an inheritance, an amount that compounded annually would be enough for her to buy his house outright. She could then use her London money to buy a shop on Milsom Street "if it is still the shopping street."

She grinned. "Yes, it is." She flung her whole arm around him and hugged him. Her face tilted toward him. It seemed the most natural thing in the world to kiss her, and so he did, taking his time to enjoy the sweet softness of her lips, the well of love and happiness rising within him.

Separating at last, they began to plan in earnest, descending to his study to write down shared information.

The dawn took them by surprise. Ramsay leaned back in his chair, watching her beloved form fade from sight, a sharp pang in his breast. This repeated leavetaking would be hard. He just prayed their plan would work.

It hadn't been easy. The bank, unwilling to give up such a huge amount of money, had drilled her through her proofs a hundred times, but at last she could afford to buy out Mrs. Marshall's lease.

To her surprise, that part was simple.

"I'm tired of living with a ghost, even if he has calmed down," Mrs. Marshall said. "Just give me some time to find a place."

With two million pounds, that wouldn't be difficult.

Jane felt compelled to write a will. She'd almost died in the past once, and without modern medicine, she wouldn't have a chance. She deeded her new house back to Mrs. Marshall and left her Bath shop to Patricia, who'd bought her out in London.

And she told Patricia the whole crazy story.

"Honey," Patricia said at last. "He might be dead, but at least he makes you happy."

\* \* \*

It was her first evening alone in Chadwick's house, her house now. She sat on their bed, the last of her trepidation gone. She couldn't wait to see him; it had been nearly three months.

Night fell, and he appeared.

Gathering her hand in his, he pressed it to his heart. "It has been too long, Jane. I almost thought—"

"It was trickier than we'd planned, but the house is mine, and I am yours." She felt a bit silly saying those words, but she needed to say the last and he needed to hear it.

"Jane, I am yours. Always."

A tingle ran down her spine. It felt like they'd committed themselves to each other, more sacred than any vow in church. "Always," she echoed in a breathy sigh.

His mouth made teasing progress down her neck, kissing soft flesh that had been forbidden to him for so long. She'd waited a long time to reach this point, and she returned the favor, kissing him wherever she could reach.

His fingers fumbled with the buttons of her old-fashioned nightgown, suddenly all thumbs. He peeled back the cotton fabric, murmuring surprised approval at her almost healed shoulder, the scars new and pink. He kissed around the periphery, invoking shudders in her. They had been so close to losing each other, losing everything.

His head bent lower to lave her sensitive skin and they lost themselves to the delicious sensations of loving.

Morning.

Jane's shoulder ached. No, it pounded with her heartbeat. She'd really overdone it last night. What had she been thinking to sleep with a guy before it had fully healed?

She didn't need to open her eyes to know Ramsay had vanished with the dawn. She knew she had to get up and get on with life in modern Bath.

It didn't matter that she'd share only his nights. After his gentle, incredible loving last night, she'd be a fool not to try and be near him, be with him.

She bit her lip. He'd given her the precious gift of self-worth and love. It was her most complicated relationship to date, but it was also without any deceit or betrayal.

*OK, time to open your eyes. Time to go.*

She blinked, glancing at the empty space in her bed where Ramsay should be.

Only.

Ramsay smiled at her, his blue gaze filled with wonder.

"But—but it's morning!" Her heart hammered against the walls of her chest.

"Yes, it is. You have slept in."

She outright stared at him. How could he be so calm about this? They were still together! "Why didn't you wake me?"

"And disturb the miracle?" His voice was suffused with choked joy. He stroked her forearm and she shivered with delight. "You're here with me."

"Are you sure you're not here with me?" She glanced at the bedside table and groaned. No alarm clock. "Oh my God." She tried to catch her breath, tried to hide her terror. It was one thing to play in the past, but another to live it. "It's 1812!" An overture began to play in her head and she started to hum it, her grin uncontrollable.

"You will miss your modern conveniences." His matter-of-fact statement seemed lost beneath his happiness. "I will be here for you and help you adapt. We've all the time in the world, after all." His smile burst into a similar grin.

She still couldn't believe it. "But how? Why now and not before?"

"I've thought about it," he said, propping himself up on the pillows and allowing the sheets to fall back from the auburn glow of his chest.

She could stare at that chest forever, the red crinkled hairs just begging to be caressed. She licked her lips, her mouth dry. When could she kiss him again? Soon, very soon. "And?"

"I think we've been fighting destiny all along. You were always meant to come back to me, to stay, only we both had to want it enough."

She'd wanted it so badly, it hurt. "And last night we did." She bent forward to kiss him. After she came up for air, she lingered, fingering the golden stubble on his cheeks. "I didn't want to wake up this morning. I didn't want to leave you."

"Hush, we're together now." He kissed her again, a sure possession of her mouth, her senses, and her soul. Just like last night, only instead of the silent bittersweet desperation of her leaving him behind in the past, he kissed her with the sweet promise of the future.

She'd miss tampons, crisps, and chocolate bars.

But it'd be worth every second.

As she bore him back down against the pillows, she felt a brief flicker of curiosity as to what the future said.

# More Regency Romance
# From Zebra